A SHORT GUIDE TO FINDING YOUR FIRST HOME IN THE UNITED STATES

An Inlandia anthology on the immigrant experience

A Short Guide to Finding Your First Home in the United States: An Inlandia anthology on the immigrant experience

ISBN: 978-1-7344977-4-8
Library of Congress Control Number: 2020950345

For permissions, write to:
Inlandia Institute
4178 Chestnut Street
Riverside CA 92501

Curated by Debra Postil
Edited by Jean Waggoner
Cover art: "Wishing Boats" by Angelique Pivoine
Book design and layout by Mark Givens

Printed and bound in the United States
Published by Inlandia Institute
Riverside, California
www.inlandiainstitute.org

A Short Guide to Finding Your First Home in the United States

An Inlandia anthology on the immigrant experience

CONTENTS

ODE TO THE RIVERSIDE CHICANO COMMUNITY

by Carlos E. Cortés

(This article is adapted from an October 6, 2020, Hispanic Heritage Month presentation for the Riverside Unified School District Board in Riverside, California.)

Thank you for the opportunity of speaking for Hispanic Heritage Month. I thought long and hard about what I should say. Latino population growth. Well, you know the story. Hispanic culture. You've heard that dozens of times. I don't want to make this Groundhog Day.

So instead I decided to tell you some stories. Stories about the local Chicano community. Stories from the perspective of an outsider.

You see, I'm not from Riverside. I arrived here in December, 1967, to become a UCR history professor. I've stayed nearly 53 years. My wife and I love it here.

As an outsider, when I think of the local Chicano community, a few words pop into my head. Historical. After all, genízaros from New Mexico settled here in the early 1840's while this land was still part of Mexico, nearly thirty years before John W. North arrived. Proud. Contributing. But especially, embracing of outsiders.

I had only been here a few weeks when I got involved in a voter registration drive led by two local Chicanas: Dee García and Jenny Gracia. They made me feel at home, a Kansas City güero with a Missouri twang.

I became the second Chicano professor in UCR history. At that time the campus had only about one hundred Chicano students. Shortly after I arrived, they formed the United Mexican American Students, which later became today's MEChA. As Chair of UCR's Chicano Studies Program for seven-and-one-half years, I worked closely with MEChA.

Then along came another outsider, Woodrow Díaz, a Puerto Rican. This was long before people talked about Latinos and Hispanics. Ethnically alone on campus, Woody asked if he could join MEChA. In embracing Riverside style, the students declared him an honorary Chicano.

In 1979 came another outsider, a Texas Chicano named Tomás Rivera. He had just been named UCR Chancellor, the first minority Chancellor in University of California history. The local Chicano community welcomed him with an enormous reception at the Riverside Convention Center.

Many people at UCR welcomed him, too, especially students and staff, who loved this gracious, open, truly authentic man. But not all of the faculty embraced him. Shortly after Tomás' first meeting with the UCR academic senate, one faculty member came to his office and shared what the professor referred to as a "really funny story." While chuckling, the professor quoted another faculty member as saying, "You know, I can understand why Governor Brown put a Chicano in as Chancellor at Riverside -- for political reasons -- but did he have to look so much like a Chicano?"

That story burrowed into Tomás' psyche. He repeated it in public lectures. Even as Chancellor, he knew that he was on ethnic probation. Five years later, in 1984, Tomás died of a heart attack. We'll never know how much the pain of ethnic probation contributed to his death.

Eight years later, in 1992, another Texas Chicano, Robert Nava -- then a Riverside Unified School District board member—proposed naming a new school after Tomás. What could be better? A tribute to an educational pioneer who had brought national visibility to Riverside. A success symbol to inspire Latino youth. Someone in whom all of Riverside could take pride. It should have been a slam dunk. Except it wasn't.

Opposition arose. Opposition from some UCR faculty. Opposition from some school board members. Surprised by this opposition, board member-elect Ofelia Valdez-Yeager asked me to speak in support of Tomás at the December 1, 1992, meeting where the final vote was to be taken. I spoke. And Tomás won. But it was a bittersweet victory. What should have been a universal celebration of inclusion had become a traumatic probationary moment for the local Chicano community.

My friend, Ellis Cose, a brilliant African American public intellectual, wrote what I consider to be the very best book on race. It's called *The Rage of a Privileged Class.* In it Ellis focuses on the experiences of educated, high-achieving, upper-middle-class African Americans. What Ellis found is that, despite their achievements, these African American success stories still encountered situations—surprising situations, shocking situations—where the color of their skin abruptly marginalized them. Despite their accomplishments and contributions, they were still on probation.

About a year ago Ellis asked me if the same thing was happening among Latinos. I said I didn't think so. I had seen Latinos angry, but I had neither witnessed nor felt the kind of deep rage that Ellis wrote about. But I had come close. At that December, 1992, school board meeting.

But what I have sensed in the Latino community is weariness. A feeling of disbelief. Of regularly being overlooked despite rapidly-growing numbers. Of being taken for granted. A sense of impatience. When will enough be enough?

Then along came Los Angeles comedian-actor Cheech Marín. A few years ago he spoke at the opening of his Chicano art exhibit in Riverside. The local Latino community lined up for hours to embrace him. Completely overwhelmed, Cheech decided that Riverside would be the perfect place to permanently house his private Chicano art collection, the nation's finest. It will be housed in the old downtown library. The entire community can take pride in it. It will help make Riverside a true destination. And yet. In the November, 2018, election one candidate made opposition to The Cheech part of his campaign. That candidate lost.

A final outsider, a Panamanian American embraced by the local Chicano community, is State Assemblyman José Medina, my former UCR student. A few years ago José launched a long-shot effort to make Ethnic Studies a California high school graduation requirement. With grit and determination, José nearly beat the odds. In August, 2020, the state legislature passed the requirement, but Governor Gavin Newsom vetoed it. However, not to worry. Like The Terminator, José's bill will be back.

I was deeply involved. In the fall of 2019 the chair of the California State Board of Education asked me if I would compose a set of ethnic studies principles to help the state deal with the enormous controversy over the original Model Ethnic Studies Curriculum report. The state liked my document well enough that it included my principles nearly verbatim in Chapter One of the revised Model Curriculum.

In developing those principles, I circulated drafts among dozens of people and met with numerous community groups. At those meetings I cautioned people that the passage of José's bill and the adoption of the Model Curriculum would be only the first steps. The real action lay with how individual school districts implemented the requirement.

At the September, 2020, Board meeting you approved a new district

Ethnic Studies graduation requirement. I'm delighted. Now I hope you'll make certain that Latinos finally get their due in that curriculum. I hope all of you accept that responsibility, individually, not just collectively.

I recognize that you represent the entire community, as it should be. But Riverside is not just a collection of random individuals. It is also a collection of communities. So, as I conclude, I appeal to each of you not only to be representatives of the district, but also to be strong advocates for those who, for far too long, have often felt on probation.

BOAT PERSON

by Angelique Pivoine

I told you I was a boat person, and you
laughed.

Holding me in your big frame,
cupping my cheeks, you said:
There's no more boat people, not since '79.
"Besides," and you kissed me on my forehead as you said that the war is over, and I survived.

I told you it always rained on my birthday,
in Saigon during the wet season,
the sky was always weeping,
and no kids would ever show up to watch me blow the candle and sing me a song.

At this you held me even tighter and promised,
we will always have cake and candle and song
because
this
is
America
California
where we are
a desert
and the sky never weeps in the desert.

At this I cried
because I forgot what my mama used to say
every wet season since 1988,
when we used to sit together on the old cherry divan,
eating cake that no one esle wanted,
and watched the teary river as it
f
 e
  l
   l
from the swirling sky onto the asphalt
spilling into our sunken home
carrying with it the dust and debris of third-world lives
and wishing boats
their hulls loaded with childhood tributes
floating down the neighborhood alley
against the onslaught of the rain
disappearing down the hungry sewers
or upstream where heaven was.

You made me our wedding ring
from gold origami paper
the way I used to make my wishing boat,
heavy with dreams, hopes, and prayers
and that was when
I remembered what my mama used to say.

"Best not expect too much happiness from life, and you'd be fine."

My mama pointed out how we all should load them light, those wishing boats,
or they would get too heavy, their paper keel dipping deeper into the water,
and disintegrate they would
sink they would
beneath the waves.

I remember what she said so clearly now,
even when it doesn't rain
here in the desert.
I remember
how my boats were always heavy,
their hulls stuffed with candies and white jasmins
red flamboyant flowers as their main sails.

Such pretty boats
and pretty wishes
but they always drowned
fell apart
in a river of tears.

Like I did
the day you left.

CHEPE Y PEPE

by Anthony Alas

"Abuelo, abuelo, abuelo! Why does your house smell like stinky feet? My precious six-year-old grandson asked.

With his appearance, an afternoon on the front porch was disturbed. My sense of tranquility crumbled up like yesterday afternoon newspaper. As a very straightforward abuelo, I saw it as my firm duty to expose my grandkids to the real world.

"Caesar, those aren't stinky feet. It's the stench of a decaying body," I said to him, with a smile.

His innocence faded with a new found jadedness. He opened his eyes in shock and curiosity.

"Wow, is it coming from abuelo Chepe? He's asleep, but nobody seems to care. They just stand over his bed. He looks a bit yellow, too," Caesar asked, with amazement.

My ice-cold Corona was sweating from the steamy August day. Caesar stood still, smiling nervously. The beer became less satisfactory. Shrugging my shoulders, I gave Caesar a forced smile.

"Your other abuelo Chepe is dying. He will drop dead soon," I replied, with cool, casual demeanor.

Tears rolled down his cheek, quite gently. He wiped his nose with the side of a charcoal hued "Ramones" t-shirt. As he sniffed and sniffed, with just a hint of drama, his big dark Aztec eyes reemerged from their shock.

"Why does it sound like there's a rattle snack in the room? He asked with unrelenting curiosity.

"That's the death rattle. It means he's very close to dropping dead. Don't feel bad; you're in the will. "Why don't you keep me alive by getting your Viejo another beer?" I said, casually.

He ran inside. Peace was restored. As I stared into the slow carefree traffic on Mission Inn Avenue, with it's backdrop of grand (and historic) craftsman, Victorian, and Spanish style homes, the heat made me quite drowsy. I took the sombrero from the side table. I placed it over my eyes for an afternoon siesta.

That lasted for a minute. A tap on the shoulder awakened me back to the sky, which instantly morphed into a muggy grey. To the left of me stood Patricia. Her salt and pepper hair had the appearance of decaying tree branches. Her black dress complimented the gloomy skies. The crucifix around her neck had a harsh redness. Most dazzling was the ice-cold Corona, she held toward me.

"Please don't have a six year old bring you a beer." She said with slight anger and amusement.

Patricia sat next to me. She took a dark lacy fan from her tan purse. I took a sip from the icy Corona. Her eyes of judgment stared me down.

"Why aren't you in there with your husband?" She asked, angrily.

As I shrugged my shoulders, I kept sipping from the ice-cold beer bottle. Music and chatter intensified. I swallowed the beer with a strong gulp.

"Too many people inside. It's not even a funeral yet, and I have to deal with a truckload of Mexican relatives, chattering and eating. I think we should let the old man die in peace." I said, hoping she would leave me alone.

"That's your husband. You should be looking after him, especially after thirty years together," she said with enthusiasm.

I drank my beer. Baffled, I didn't know quite what to say. That nervous feeling raced through me. Starvation and bloat from the beer created remarkable sound effects. I tried hard to hold back vicious gases.

"Maybe I don't love him after thirty years. Maybe I'm too fat and old for my silver fox's taste. I thought he liked gordos. He's the typical man. I hope his dick turns green before he goes unconscious."

Patricia swiftly lit up a cigarette. The porch had the scent of nicotine and Mexican bread baking. The nostalgic scent brought me back to parties, which Chepe and I reveled in. Annoyed, I longed to be alone. Typically, there would be zero embarrassment with telling Patricia to scram. However, with Chepe on his deathbed, a certain sense of pathos overcame my spicy temper.

"Patty, why do you insist on smoking when we have a man dying of lung cancer, just feet away?" I asked, rather annoyed.

"I smoke when I'm nervous," she replied, her right hand shaking slightly.

Irritated, I avoided conversation with her. She was quite eager to speak. However, that cigarette smoke would clog up her vocal cords.

"That burial plot came in handy," Patricia asked, with a wink.

As she uttered those words, an attractive gay male couple jogged past my home. My eyes met with the handsome blonde, blue-eyed gringo and his twenty-something dark eyed, dark haired Latin lover. They fit the physical ideals idolized by mainstream culture.

"Pepe, tu pipi no esta verda (Pepe, your penis isn't green, yet)," laughed, Patricia.

I rolled my eyes. The couple symbolized the perfect exterior that I dreamed of as a young man in El Distictro Federal. Happy, healthy, and affluent was the ideal.

However, Chepe and I only had a brief time. A sense of disappointment overcame me.

"Chepe certainly didn't have any problems in that dept. He drove around downtown with that gringo boy, who looked a bit like a young Paul Newman." I replied, as my beer was chugged quickly and nervously.

"How do you know that it wasn't just a friend? a student? a transient?" Patricia asked, naively.

"An old man that wrinkly does not have a man that handsome, without some sort of compensation. " I replied.

Disappointment kicked me in the culo, again. Cono, the only way I'll be reunited with Chepe is through death. Gracias, Senior for that coffin burial plot. Even in the afterlife, I'll be on top.

"Don't you think it's a bit of karma, Pepe? You took my man and burial plot, " said Patricia.

I spit out my last sips of Corona. It formed into a tiny boozy river along the porch's darkened mahogany wood.

"Your husband? Aren't you a lesbiana? If it weren't for Chepe's double life, you would've stayed a miserable esposa. No Home Depot trips, no lesbiana week in Palm Springs, no Yolanda. You love Yolanda. She has the goodies you like," I said, with a few giggles.

Stunned, Patricia leaned back on the floral chair. She stared at the multicolored birdhouses hanging from the ceiling. They swayed in the wind, and resembled the rainbow flag, ironically.

"That may be true, but I fell in love with the person. It just took fifteen shots of Patron to conceive Anita," she replied.

We laughed. The screen door opened quickly. Anita appeared. Her floral summer dress accentuated an Aztec skin tone. Her long black hair nearly touched her hips. She looked like a Latina goddess.

"Mama, Yolanda is bored" Anita replied.

"What? Is the stench of death not entertaining enough?" I answered.

Immediately, Patricia leapt from her chair. She signaled me to go inside with her. I shook my head, no. She persisted, then her eyes nearly popped out of their sockets, with frustration. Her eyes were raised to the heavens. Aggressively, she entered the house.

Anita stood above me, her arms folded. I looked away from her. The perfectly manicured lawns and restored homes provided more comfort. High heels tapped. The euphoria of a quiet afternoon became a lost cause.

"Papa, aren't you going to go inside, and spend some time with your hubby?" She asked, sternly.

Disco balls, love making in a Puerto Vallarta hotel, the beautiful wedding ceremony we shared, it caused a spark of nostalgia. Nostalgia caused me to consider taking a last look. Then my mind was further laced with different emotions.

Frustrated, I threw my sombrero on the ground. Flashbacks came through my mind. A shut door, an ambulance, an induced coma, the home hospice arrangements became as common (in my life) as a café con leche, in the mornings.

Anger birthed itself from frustration. I then remembered the bitter times. The separate bedrooms, infidelity, and fat shamming, Chepe would not be missed. I questioned my own humanity. Was I terrible person for having fallen out of love with my husband?

"Anita, I'm not going in. Sorry, I'm mad, and I'm going to stay mad," I replied.

Her darkened skin reddened. Red veins of sadness surrounded those big brown eyes. Catholic guilt kicked me in the cojones. Terribly guilty, I watched Anita walk back inside the house.

The sun re-appeared from the gloomy afternoon. A white truck drove by. As it slowed down, I stared in wonder. The window rolled down. A gentleman with salt and pepper hair, hazel eyes, and white smile, waved.

"Hola, Chepe," he gleefully yelled from the car.

"Hola, Antonio," I replied.

The attraction was uncanny. As an overweight, traditionally awkward looking man, I defied the tradition of the Latin lover. However, through Antonio's eyes, I encountered the love and lust, which first drew me to Chepe. The idea of being a merry widow was somewhat daunting, even in our tumultuous relationship.

After careful thinking, I took a deep breath. I picked up the sombrero from the floor, and placed it on my head. Bravely, I headed inside.

Our old home had been dimly lit. Green walls, quirky paintings of the Catholic saints and cats, retro-grey couches contrasted its less funky Craftsman architecture. Livelier than the eclectic décor were the family members, who chatted and ate Mexican staples. Cumbia music blasted.

Since everyone became preoccupied with chatter, my entrance was given little attention. I opened the tall wooden door. Chepe's death rattle drowned out the lively music. Anita sat, staring at Chepe. Tears ran down her cheek. As Anita leapt from the chair, she gave me a shy smile.

I took Anita's seat. Folding my arms, I sat staring at Chepe's head, which rocked from side to side. Tubes and medical equipment blended into the drab bedroom. Finally, he turned. His eyes opened. My eyes lacked emotion as he stared at me. Bigger, and bigger his eyes grew. Did I look like Satan or something?

The words "te amo" couldn't bounce out of my drunken vocal cords. Chepe opened his eyes one last time, and went back to his coma-induced sleep. The two Mexican boys in love would become a memory. Then I questioned our own years. As he continued to sleep, I walked out of the room. He liked his own bedroom, and didn't want to be disturbed. Chepe was going to that massive gay discoteca in the sky.

The END.

Originally published in *Scribble Lit*.

MY TIA TILLY

by Juanita E. Mantz

Mom took us out of school today so that we could go with her to visit our Aunt Tilly. Mom does this every so often because she hates driving to Orange County by herself. We don't mind missing school. On the way there, we make faces at people through the dusty windows of Mom's brown Pinto station wagon. My twin Jackie occasionally flips people off and I elbow her in the side, trying to get her to stop. I catch Mom's stare in the rearview mirror as she screams, "Cut it out girls!" We know to stop or else risk her reaching backwards to slap at us from the front seat.

Even when we are not goofing off, driving with Mom is always dangerous, she drives erratically, telling people off as she goes. "Jerk!" she'll yell when someone cuts her off, honking her horn at least twice at them. We have to pinch each other to keep from laughing out loud. Mom hates semi-trucks, she actually closes her eyes if they get too close, like right now.

"Mom!" I yell, "Be careful, the truck is..."

Mom turns around and glares me into silence before I can finish my sentence. At least her eyes are open.

"Ayyyyy," Aunt Tilly says as she opens the door to her small three bedroom house in Buena Park. The house is covered in pink stucco and has large plastic flowers in the garden that spin. As I plop down on the plastic covered sofa to read my book, she croons, "Flaca Jennie, gordita Jackie y bonita Annie."

You know tias, they have to differentiate us, it would be too easy to say, there goes Judy's little girls. Instead Tia Tilly has to fit into little boxes: the skinny bookworm ("Jenny, mija, get your head out of the book and eat something, I made some rice"), the chubby middle child and black sheep ("tttt tttt ttttt Jackie, slow down, save some for the rest of us, Judy, you gotta watch this one, she's got John's white gordo genes") and the youngest, perfect one ("oh, Annie, come here bonita").

Just for the record, and there will be no dispute about this, Tilly is crazy but we all love her despite this. She smokes a cigarette every five minutes. She just lit up and I can see the smoke rising like fog from the butt she just snuffed out a minute ago. She has five Siamese cats, which sit throughout the house perched on tall tan cat tower scratching posts. Tilly loves her cats, especially Tabitha, the most evil one, who hisses at anyone who tries to pet her. Years later, Tabitha will bite the tip of Tilly's finger off and as the story goes, Tilly will put the little piece of finger in a Dixie cup cover it with ice and take it with her to the hospital where the doctors will sew it back on. Tilly will keep the cat.

Tilly always wears a robe with pink backgrounds and purple flowers, she calls the robe her house dress. With her blond hair piled on top of her head, she looks like a poorer version of Mrs. Roper from Three's Company. She is a weda, but you can't tell because she tans and speaks fluent Spanish and cooks delicious Mexican food. Tilly has a laugh like a wild horse and a dying hyena put together.

Right now, even though I can't hear what they're saying, I can tell by the way Tilly is laughing that she and Mom are reliving their days growing up next door to each other around the corner from Knott's Berry Farm, back when it was still a real farm. Mom always says that it was a simpler time and I can tell that talking about the olden days makes them feel younger.

Tilly met Mom at a bus stop when they were fourteen years old and Tilly ended up marrying my mom's brother Frank, who everyone calls Poncho. Poncho is the second oldest of Mom's many brothers. Tilly and Mom's conversations vacillate between Spanish and English. When they speak Spanish, they think we don't understand, but we can usually figure it out.

Mom is hunched over the dining table, stirring her coffee, alternating sips with laughter. She's laughing so hard that I can see the back of her throat. She never laughs like this at home. It makes me smile to see her happy.

Mom is a different person at Aunt Tilly's house. She seems calmer here, probably because she's not chasing after and screaming at Dad. I can almost picture her and Tilly as their younger teenage selves. They talk about how they had dirt floors back tin the day and all the crazy stuff they used to do. They would go on double dates and Tilly would sneak into Poncho's room late at night. They talk about how Mom was the only brown girl in her class. They talk about my Dad's carousing.

"It's those Montana cowboys," Tilly says with a cackle. You should have married brown like I did."

The best part of our visit is when they bring out the photo albums. My sisters and me lean over the table, taking pictures off the sticky backing of the photo album. I look Mom in her sixth grade photo, she is probably about the same age I am right now. She has a sharp overbite and in the black and white photo, her dark skin stands out against the whiteness of her classmates. Mom doesn't talk much about that time. All she says was that it was hard not knowing how to speak English well.

Other than looking at the photo album out, there is not much to do at Tilly's house. Tilly and Poncho have three kids, Quetay, Richard and Tina, and they are at school. It's so boring here. I try to read my book, but Jackie and Annie won't let me. We try to watch TV, but Tilly likes to keep it on the Spanish channel and we don't speak Spanish very well at all. A fat man in a bumblebee suit is dancing on the screen right now and I giggle in unison with my sisters.

When we leave Tilly's house, Mom takes us to Huntington Beach. It's our favorite part of going to Orange County and makes the long drive and hours of boredom at Tilly's house well worth it. We get excited when we smell the salt in the air and start screaming, which causes Mom to wince. As soon as she parks, we jump out of the car and race to find a spot on the sand to put our bath towels. Mom lays out her blanket. Annie walks down to the waters' edge to gather shells. I watch as Annie carefully washes each shell before putting it in her plastic bucket. She's just as careful with the shells as she is with her dolls. I bury Jackie in the sand, which she loves. The waves get bigger and bigger and Jackie jumps up and grabs my hand and we speed into the water to wash off, jumping up and down with the rhythm of the surf.

Mom sits on the beach reading her True Story magazine. Mom hates the water even more than a cat does, maybe because she never learned how to swim. We shout, "Come in mom! C'mon!" She ignores us and continues reading, munching on the peanut butter and jelly crackers Tilly packed for her.

Once we are covered in salt and sea, my sisters and me lie down on the beach towels to get a tan and dry off our suits. After a while and without warning, Mom says with a scowl, "Let's go girls." Mom has the same frown she always gets when she wonders where Dad is. I know it's time to go home but I don't want to leave. When we get home I know a fight will be brewing, just like it always is, and I want to stay here in the sun.

A NICE BOY

by Raffi Boyadjian

"Oh, dear!"

The tall, thin man wearing a brown hat crashed into me in the crowded airport; spilling me, my comic books and my colored pencils across the floor. My chin throbbed from smashing it on the hard ground.

"Are you ok, son?"

I didn't understand a word as he lifted me off the floor and picked up my books and pencils. His voice had a lilt to it, like a glissando. I liked the sound, but I just stood there silently, noticing moist blue eyes under arched eyebrows. He reminded me of Opa. I already missed him. I missed everyone, terribly.

"Are you ok?"

He kept standing there. I started to worry that he was angry, though his expression belied that. I dared not rub my chin, lest it set him off. He noticed that my comic books weren't in English.

"Ah. German?"

He pointed at me.

"Dootch?"

I nodded. My mother returned from the luggage carousel with our suitcases. I ran to her and grabbed her hand. He handed my things to my mother and apologized.

"I'm afraid I knocked your son over. I'm very sorry."

My mother answered in halting English.

"He iz ok."

The man pulled a dollar out of his pocket and crouched down to my height to hand it to me. I looked at the strange bill.

"Zay sank you."

I looked up at her, not understanding the instruction.

"Sag danke."

"Danke."

"You're welcome."

He patted my head and then rushed off, waving over his shoulder.

I rubbed my chin as I examined the bill. It was green and white and warm. I held it against my cheek. It smelled musty. My mother grabbed the suitcases and headed down the corridor to join my father, brother and sister in the customs office.

"Komm schon, kindchen."

I hopped and ran trying to keep pace; trying to avoid swinging suitcases.

We entered a small office still decorated for Christmas. A small silver aluminum tree with large blinking lights sat on top of a grey file cabinet. Two red paper bells in opposite corners and a long gold garland connecting them framed the otherwise bare far wall. It seemed hardly cheery. The man talking to my father reminded me of the bald sidekick in *The Great Race*. I watched the movie with my uncles and aunts in Höchst, the week before we left. I laughed until tears rolled down my face. Especially during the pie throwing scene. My father motioned to my mother.

"Heer ees."

My mother took over signing paperwork, while my father dealt with my fidgeting infant sister who'd just awoken and started crying. My brother stood next to his chair, with his arms wrapped around my father's leg.

"What is the nature of your visit?"

"Ve arr nut visiteeng. Ve arr leeveeng heer."

"You're leaving?"

"No. Ve arr komming heer."

"You're returning from a trip?"

"Ach… nein. Ve hov movet heer."

"Oh. You're moving here?"

"Ja! Yes."

"Hmm. Customs gave me the wrong information."

He ripped up the forms my mother had been signing and pulled new ones out of his desk. My father frowned.

"Was ist loss?"

She shushed him.

"Do you have your visas?"

"Ja."

She handed them over. He held up my mother's and father's while checking their faces against the pictures.

"This man is your husband?"

"Yes."

"How long have you been married?"

"Ayt yeaz."

He bent forward to fill in the information on the forms. The blonde fuzz on top of his head looked like the fuzz on top of my sister's head.

"These are your children?"

"Yes."

He held up our visas and to match our faces.

"How old are they?"

"Von, feif und zex yeaz oold."

He winked at me as he handed the visas back. I clutched my comics close to my chest. My mother stroked my hair and whispered that I should tell the man what she taught me in Germany. I shook my head.

"Bitte."

"I EM eh NAYSE BOYee."

My cheeks burned red hot. My mother beamed at her polyglot son.

"I'm sure you are, kid."

He handed me a candy from the same drawer in his desk. I put it in my mouth, then spat it out. Butterscotch. What a cruel trick. My father smacked my head.

My head hurt. Not merely from the smack, or the fall. The unfamiliarity of everything , the bright lights made my temples throb and my eyes burn. The cacophony of beeping trams and rolling luggage and rushing travelers and staccato announcements over intercoms… I hated it here. I missed my uncles and aunts and Oma and Opa. I missed my friends. How was I going to make friends here when I couldn't understand anyone? Everybody talked like they were chewing gum. *Ngow, ngow…* I bit my lip to keep from crying. I failed. Which set my sister off again. Which angered my father. My mother snatched my sister from him and sealed our fate with a flourish of her wrist. She slid the forms over to my father to countersign. It was then, with those signatures, that I realized that my parents wouldn't look out for me. The packing, the goodbyes, even the flight over - it all seemed reversible, but this action was indelible. The epiphany started me sobbing. My brother joined in, making it a trio.

"Verdammt noch mal!"

My father picked up my brother and yanked me hard, towards the door. My mother apologized to the man as he handed back our visas.

"Dey arr verry teyered."

He nodded. The door closed. My father, brother and I stood in the bright hallway. I could still hear my sister cry over my own wailing. It sounded like she was being rocked: *"Aa-yaa-yaa."* My father jerked my arm. He glowered down at me. I stopped crying immediately; though my shoulders still convulsed as I sniffled.

"Halt's maul!"

My brother stopped crying as well; knowing that it was the prudent thing to do. My father sighed angrily and lit a cigarette. He ran his hands through his hair as it dangled between his lips. It burned down to the filter before the door opened again and my mother came out with my sister. She'd stopped crying and was sucking her thumb.

"Welcome to the United States."

"Sank you verry match."

"Vertig?"

My mother ignored my father's question. Instead she handed him the paperwork along with my sister. She picked up my brother. I took her hand as we headed down the long hallway towards our connecting flight to our new life. I looked up at her as a tear hit my forehead.

MOSCATERO

by Antonio Lopez

They bathe in the standing puddles
of an Elephant's Foot.

Rainfall slicked off las palmas,
where mosquitoes rest their nose-daggers
brimmed with blood-drenched chupe,
loaded sangrias, cock-
tails which help them glide through
the propina-fueled nights.

They drudge off la cruda
by perching on the meat racks

of Don Jaramillo's ear, el dueño de la casa
and whisper to him, "Ándale jefe.
Déjenos quedar otro ratito."

He stirs from a sagging hammock,
swatter-palm whizzes the air, but gets caught
in the limping clothesline overhead,
where he hangs his favorite guayabera.

He exhales.
Chest sags like worn-out boxing gloves.

Las moscas' wings are shattered glass,
tiny oars to wade through the wind,

to skid row past the backyard selva,
where they prolly filmed *Apocalypto.*

Shhh. Se oye—
when el tráfico dies down,
when los techadores stop
their steel-toe zapateada—
su historia.

The leaned back coupe for decades
filled on premium "échele ganas."
Yonke-doctors pace its tawny flesh,
Oakley shades x-ray

el estandard que no funciona
los rosarios a few beads short,
the Coke 2 liters stripped of their label—
water containers for las labores.

La juventud hardware, stripped to chassis
which can't get a Cat Scan
'cuz la seguranza ya no lo cubre.

These larvae
are children of la choza.

Outhouse brown-prints
where they first sprouted
their legs off a sofa's armrest,

and spat mounds of carcajadas con mamá,
as they spend the last drips of su velada watching
El Gendarme Desconocido, where el comandante
yells to México's querido payaso
"¡Con más cargo señor! ¡CON MAS CARGO!"

Cantinflas marches in beltless fatigues.

These larvae
hide under Master's brimmed fedora,
as he trembles an oak'd fist to the city inspector
who gives a third warning for the fly-gathering trees.

A multa of six months pension,

but el Don pokes the man's state-issued lanyard,
y grita his last muela, "Tú no sacarás
ningún centavo de mí."

These larvae
earn their pupa
while incubated dentro papá's jacket,
brawny thorax that shields the sun
in a soft whool.

Nuzzled under fleece-flaps, their hardened shells
chip under every earth-shattering
cough and pruned vein.

Sobriety is when the field's calor
dries wings once drenched in the wine-songs
that haunted their fathers.

Cuando el Don se duerma,
they'll crawl out of his broken zipper
and take flight, sawing through the taut skin
de la madrugada.

WHITE GIRL

by Juanita E. Mantz

"She's a white girl, but I'm living with a white girl.
She's a white girl, but I'm living with a white girl."

—X-White Girl

I was in second grade at Mariposa Elementary when one of the Mexican girls at school called me white girl. I knew she was wrong. I wasn't a white girl. I saw myself as Mexican with some white thrown in. My Mexican mom grew up middle class in Orange County. Mom loved country music and cowboys and met my German dad at a honky tonk bar. My dad grew up dirt poor in Montana and loved country music, drinking and fiery, brown women. Mom was not the first of his four wives, but she was his last.

The white girls saw me as Mexican and thought I should hang with the girls they called "the cholas". Most of the so-called cholas were Mexican girls who wore karate slip-on shoes with fitted pants and black jackets.

One of my favorite people in the world at the time was my older cousin Carol from Buena Park who some considered a chola. I would have liked to hang out with the cholas. Yet, I knew I didn't fit in because I was a nerd, preppie girl who always sat at the front of the class and the so called cholas made fun of me for not speaking Spanish.

I was never lonely because I had my twin sister Jackie to hang out with at breaks (they had put us in separate classes by this time).

In second grade, I met Melinda, who everyone called Mel. Mel was a clotheshorse and she made fun of the cholas' outfits behind their backs. Mel was born in Mexico and spoke Spanish and despite her disdain, the cholas accepted her. Mel hung out with different groups depending on her mood. That is, until we met and became best friends.

"Everyone says you're smart," Mel said with a smile. "But what are you wearing?" she said with a raised eyebrow as she stared at the green frog t-shirt that I had paired with blue flared Dittos. The outfit had seemed like a good idea that morning.

Mel shopped at Mervyn's and she made a face when I told her that my mom shopped for our clothes at K-Mart. Everyone wanted to be friends with Mel and I desperately wanted her to like me. She was everything I was not. She had straight black hair that she wore spiked up and perfect bronze colored skin. She favored jean jackets and tight jeans and even back then in elementary school, she was the epitome of cool. Mel was also bossy and sarcastic and popular with the boys. When she invited my twin Jackie and I over her house after school, I tried to act nonchalant by saying, "sure" when I felt like screaming "yes". Mom forced us to let our younger sister Annie tag along because it turned out that Mel had a little sister named Pam that was Annie's age.

Mel and Pam lived with their parents in an apartment down the street from us in Ontario. Mel's mom Mary was in her early twenties and lonely because she didn't drive and Mel's dad Arturo was always at work. After a couple of visits, Mary started watching my sisters and me almost every day because Mom didn't want us home alone after school while she worked the split shift (Mom called it the fuck you over shift) at a local Chinese restaurant.

As an after school treat, Mary would make us posole soup with home-made tortillas on the side which was a sharp change from the prepackaged macaroni and cheese Mom made us or the stews and beef roast that Dad cooked.

"Sientate," Mary would say and all us girls would crowd around her tiny kitchen table slurping our bowls of soup. After our snack, we would walk to the liquor store on the corner to buy the salted plums covered with chili powder that Mel had introduced us to.

Mary and Mom became friends. If Mom got off early, she would come by and sit with Mary in the kitchen drinking cup after cup of coffee talking in Spanish. Mel would make me laugh by mimicking how Mom put spoon after spoon of sugar in her coffee. If Mom didn't get off early, Dad would pick us up when he got off his shift at Mayflower Moving Company. Dad was often late and would drive up in his pickup truck with the smell of beer on his breath. Mary would shake her head and say, "John you're burracho. Can you drive?"

Dad would wave her off and load us into the car swerving to Johnny

Cash the four blocks home.

I didn't bring friends home because if Mom was having a bad day she would tell people off. Mel and Pam became the exception to that rule because Mel handled Mom's varying moods with ease and didn't react when Mom yelled.

Mel and I didn't talk about race at all. We knew we were brown. That was obvious. I loved hearing Mel talk Spanish to her mom even though Mel was hesitant to do so. She wanted her mom to learn English. But, I was jealous of this other world of rolled out Rs.

If asked, Mom would say that she didn't teach us Spanish because Dad hated when Mom's brothers made fun of him in Spanish. My uncles called Dad "barracho güero" which we knew meant drunk white man. In truth, Mom's reasons for withholding her native tongue were much more complicated. Mom was the only non-white girl in her Orange County elementary school class. Years later, Mom showed me her black and white elementary school photo and she looked like a small dark spot in a class of white faces.

Mom looked at the picture and shook her head with a frown and said, "It was hard being the only Mexican girl. They didn't let you speak Spanish."

I knew, even at a young age, that color mattered. Annie was sixteen months younger than us and she had Dad's lighter coloring. People would always coo over her and say how pretty she was. All my relatives called Annie bonita.

When I was in fifth grade, Mom decided her girls needed to be in Catholic school and we were upset because we would have to make new friends. Despite our protests, Mom enrolled us at St. George's in Ontario, a run down Catholic school. Mom promised we could visit Mel and Pam on the weekends. When the school found out that Mom waitressed, they gave her a low income discount charging her one hundred dollars a month tuition for all three of us. Even with the discount, the tuition was still a stretch and Mom struggled to buy us faded, used uniforms with her tips. We complained the whole summer before school started. Mom told us that we were ungrateful brats that needed to stop bitching.

The first months were hard in a new school. The nuns were stern and church was mandatory every day. And, I had to play volleyball, which I was inept at. No matter how hard I tried, I couldn't hold my arms right to bounce the ball off my wrist and I always ducked whenever the ball came at me.

In sixth grade, Laura McPherson, who was the captain of the volleyball team, invited Jackie and me to a slumber party at her house. Laura's dad was a doctor and everyone knew she was rich. She lived in a huge Spanish style house.

There was a girl in our class who always made fun of me. I don't remember her name. All I remember was that she was chubby with blonde hair. We got into a fight at the slumber party and she called me a spic wetback. I screamed back at her, "Fuck you you fat bitch, my dad's white." I knew spic was a racial slur, but I didn't know what it meant. I knew what wetback meant. I had heard Dad's friends use the insult. Mom hated those friends of his. Mom said Dad's friends were a bunch of white trash drunks who were a bad influence on Dad.

The spic and wetback slurs stuck in my mind during my time at St. George's. I would sometimes look down at my faded uniform and wish it was bright and new and the right length instead of long and faded. When Mom put us back in public school for our seventh grade year, I was relieved. I wanted to hang out with Mel and ride bikes with her after school and go to the liquor store. I felt comfortable with her. Mel knew my dad was a white drunk man and that my mom was Mexican and crazy. She didn't care and neither did I.

It is thirty-five years later and Mel and I are still best friends. Last week, I stopped by at her small apartment in Rancho Cucamonga and ate her homemade posole while our moms drank wine and laughed and reminisced.

"Remember Judy, when the girls got drunk and Mel came home with only one shoe," Mary said to Mom.

"I remember when the girls stole John's pickup truck and drove around the neighborhood at night," Mom said with a shrug.

"They were locas," Mary said and Mom nodded in agreement.

I brought them coffee and watched as Mom spooned spoon after spoon of sugar in her coffee. Mel looked at me and smiled and I tried not to laugh.

I felt right at home.

KNOCKERS AND BOOSTERS

by Judy Kronenfeld

"Ah, those days in New York when I met my girlfriends and went to the theater," Mother sighs like an opera star in her lawn chair behind me, still talking at Mrs. Rivera.

I'm standing two inches from the sideline, *my* mind on the last quarter of the soccer game. Don't know why Eddie and I always drag her—ever since her and Pops moved out here next to their inland SoCal kin. The "delight of her life," her "precious granddaughter, a Blue Birdy, a regular atleet." Ha. The coach has Janey playing forward for the first time. Could Mother care less? Right up there with Tracy. Lupe with the thunder thighs and Tanisha gotta hold the defense—

Damn! Charlene, the Rainbows' superstar, just charged right past her. But Janey's playing her position. O.K. *O.K.* 95 pounds of solid muscle, not an ounce of flab, except for a pinch around her middle she gets from her father—Eddie's not exactly Mr. Svelte. But that'll come off this summer in soccer camp. Which she's gonna love. O.K. Lupe picks up one of her pillars and booms the ball out of bounds. O.K.

"We'd hop a bus, stop for a cup of coffee, a cheese danish, then off we'd go, Broadway, off-Broadway. Busy. Busy."

Theater? What theater? We didn't go *nowhere* cause Mother was always doing the closets, unloading them, tarpapering for the umpteenth time, spraying with Flit, you know.

"But now, Harold, he won't budge," she says. Pops, like always, has given up on the chair he plunked down a safe distance from her, and is stomping up and down the sideline, making holes in the ground with his cane.

"I know what you mean," says Mrs. Rivera. She's Lupe's grandma.

I step back a couple of inches so I can hear them a little clearer behind me. My shorts give me a tug—I've put on a little middle-age spread.

"Carlos, también. Bezball, hockey, soccer, futball, wrestling. Anything on the tube."

"Eee-yucch," says Mother. "I hate all that slugging and hitting and killing each other."

That's why she sent me to "Summer Fun at the Metropolitan Museum" when I was nine, instead of Girl Scout camp—putting on the dog, as if she came over from the old country with a whole bunch of arty-farties in steerage. Until I finally put my foot down. And then it was too late. There is *nothing* worse than coming up to bat at the all-star softball game, the whole camp staring at you, when you've never held a bat before. I shove my hand down my pocket and get my shorts out of the cleft of my behind. Gotta remember this brand is cut weird.

Five minutes into the fourth quarter, still 2-1, Rainbows. "C'mon sweethearts," Eddie yells, his fists clenched, "keep up the pressure!" Pops waves his cane and croaks "Yeah! Janey! Knock 'em dead!" The batteries in Mother's hearing aid must be dead.

"Now that town had *life*," Mother says. "If you know what I mean."

If you like what creeps out from dark corners.

The Rainbows' goalie is fumbling the ball. I stomp my foot in frustration, can't help it.

"I know what you mean," says Mrs. Rivera. What do they care? Janey, pay attention! Lupe's running up too far—what does she think she's gonna do? Damn! The goalie throws herself on it, she's got it. Drop-kick.

"It's so quiet in this town. No-one on the street. Drive here. Drive there. Life," she says.

Here's life. Janey zooms in on the ball, takes on a halfback. Gorgeous! What a foot on that kid! Not a powerhouse like Lupe, but in the right spot. After camp, there'll be the regular season again, then, who knows, maybe Select. She's good enough. Oops, she's sliding right down, got the wind knocked right out of her.

"What ya waitin' for, girl," someone says.

"Get up, honey! Hang tough!" Eddie shouts.

"Oh my God, someone's hurt," Mother shrieks. She looks up in time to see Lupe run up and take charge.

"Way to go, Lupe!" her dad yells.

"Isn't she dragging her foot a little," Mother says in my general direction. Like she hadn't noticed before when Lupe was at our house. Like I hadn't told her something or other happened to it when the Riveras waded across some ditch on the border near Tijuana. "A pity," she even said, shaking her wattles. And I could see she was thinking "An alligator? One of those fish with teeth?"

I turn around and give her a look that could kill; she looks back at me like she has no idea what I mean.

"As I was saying. Life," Mother says. I know she's got her elbow on the arm of the chair, her thumb and middle finger in a little circle, and her ample arm is shaking like she's got Parkinson's.

"I know what you mean," says Mrs. Rivera.

"The Schubert, the Provincetown Playhouse, the Village—"

"México, también," says Mrs. Rivera.

"The Metropolitan Opera House, the City Center Ballet—"

"The Ballet Folklorico," says Mrs. Rivera.

"Carnegie Hall—"

"El Teatro de los Insurgentes," says Mrs. Rivera.

"Fifth Avenue, the people, the shops," says Mother.

"Ay—El Paseo de la Reforma—"

"But they fall in love, they get married, they move away," says Mother.

"Si, amor," says Mrs. Rivera. And she starts to sing a song with a lot of la's, quiero, la la la something or other.

"Love, shmuv," says Mother. I just know she's eyeing Eddie, belly hanging out of his pants.

I don't hear anything from Mrs. Rivera. I sneak a look. Her head is lolling on her shoulder; her mouth is open, drooling a little.

"Pass it, pass it," Eddie's screaming. Tanisha's being crowded out by a Rainbows halfback with hippo hips. And ther-r-re's Janey. She backs up, sticks her little foot in, and poof—the ball's out of there. Oops, hippo hips backs up and gets it. Amazing she can move so fast.

"Don't just stand there, Blue Babes!" Eddie yells, beating his fists on his thighs. Lupe moves in on hippo hips, booms it. Janey almost—shit. Tracy's got it. She's taking it down! The goalie's too far out. It's in! Lupe's dad gives Eddie five and spins around. "Way to play, way to play," he shouts.

"Someone made a goal," Mother says, her arm on Mrs. Rivera's lawn chair.

"What I had in mind for Roberta," Mother says, like I'm not standing ten feet in front of her, hopping up and down, but dozing like Mrs. Rivera, "was somebody refined, somebody who likes exhibits, shows, nice restaurants, not a klutz who sits around in front of the tube all Saturday with his hand in his pants."

JEEzus.

Janey kicks off. She loses it. Big booming kick from the Rainbows. Three minutes left.

"I use to imagine him," Mother says. "An orthodontist maybe, or a C.P.A.—*real* refined. He pulls out her chair at restaurants, he bows his head toward her while she talks, he turns to their friends, his hand on the back of her chair, a little smile on his face, like he's thinking, 'My *wife*.' Gorgeous!"

Pops stomps by in front of her chair. She makes a big show of clearing her throat, coughs and spews—probably into that handkerchief she stores in her sleeve.

Mrs. Rivera must of woke up again. "Me and Carlos, we use to walk around el zócalo," she mumbles. But she still sounds like she's dreaming. "He stand so tall, hold my arm in his. Or we sit, todo el día, en los confidentes, sabes? Para los novios."

Mother is silent. So maybe *now* she can pay attention to superstar Charlene, who's got the ball and looks like business. Uh, oh, breakaway, breakaway. DEfense! There's Lupe, and Charlene's down! "Lupe, Lupe, Lupe," everyone roars. "Gracias a Dios," I think I hear Mrs. Rivera say. The ref runs up, shakes a yellow card in front of Lupe. The coach shrugs. "Who's foul?" mother says, trying to catch my eye. Charlene takes the penalty kick, but it falls short.

Now Janey's breaking toward the goal, looking for a pass. Watch the offsides, Janey, watch thc offsides! She's got the ball, she's trying for the score. Mother throws me one of her triumphant looks just as the ref calls the offsides. Across the field, the crowd is whooping it up. "Open your eyes next time, skinny!" someone calls out. Mother wobbles upright and claps her hands. "That's my girl! Yay Blue Birds! Knock 'em dead" she screams while the Rainbows score on a quick pass from the penalty kick, 3-2, shit!

"You can do it, you can do it, there's still time!" Lupe's Dad yells. And, Janey's got it and sending it way back to Lupe who sends it to Tracy, and it's in, wow! Where'd they learn to pass like that? Everyone is hopping up and down. Pops drops his cane and hugs me. Eddie hugs Lupe's Mom. Lupe's Dad hugs me. The whistle blows. Pops hugs Eddie. Eddie hugs me. Lupe's Mom hugs Lupe's Dad.

"Is the game over?" Mother says, sitting down.

The teams line up and file past each other, slapping hands. Mrs. Rivera holds out her arms for Lupe. Lupe puts her head in her grandma's lap and squeezes her round the middle. Mother takes a good gander, then nods slantwise at me, eyes cast up to heaven under her wrinkled brow, her thumb ready to hitch a ride, making like "Wudya believe?"

The nerve! "Mo-om—" I growl. I can feel the veins in my head popping. My teeth are sanding each other.

"Ssh!" she says, tipping her head toward Mrs. Rivera.

Now I'm gonna throttle her. Real good too this time, too. Or go over to Lupe's grandma and tell her what a great game Lupe played. But Janey is bounding off the field. So I don't.

"Way to go," Eddie says, grabbing her around the neck.

"That's my girl," Pops says, slapping her on the back. "Chip off the old block."

"What did I say," Mother says. "Could they have done it without you? Kiss?" and she holds out her cheek. Janey kisses her, too.

"You did great," I say, squeezing in, putting my hands on her shoulders and kissing her salty forehead.

"Great game, sweethearts," Eddie says to the last Blue Babes streaming off the field, giving Janey's hand a last squeeze.

"Really, it was—a great game," I say, linking my arm in her arm.

"Touché," says Pops, picking up her free hand, and giving it a kiss, with a bow. Since when did he get so courtly? What I remember is "Behave! Or you'll get a smack in the face with the back of my hand."

"Look at that sweat," Mother says. "A real atleet." She dabs at Janey's face with a tissue, then rummages again in her purse, holds up a lemon drop. "Candy for energy?" I could tell her where to put that.

"C'n I save it for later, grams?" Janey pockets the lemon drop and pushes through the crowd of us. She pops a Coke from Lupe's mom's cooler and tears the waxed paper off a churro.

"Do you really...?" I ask, thinking of soccer camp.

"What?" Janey asks, her mouth full of sugar.

"Nothing," I say.

This story first appeared in *Wilshire Review*, Number 5 (2001), and has since been very slightly edited.

SPILLING THE BEANS

by Natalie Hirt

The pot of beans had been simmering all morning as everyone in the house prepared for a picnic at the church. My house was wonderful in bean smell, roasted chilies, and Grandma's famous rice. It smelled even better than the burrito factory down the street. Way better.

Mama's bedroom was sticky with Aqua Net hairspray as she and my aunties and cousins filled up the room to get ready for the picnic. I stood behind the door tucked in the corner, trying to ignore the comments about my big eyebrows and how much I looked like my father.

"She's light, but she didn't get his blue eyes."

"No, but she sure got his eyebrows!" Then gales of giggles. I couldn't open my mouth to defend myself because then they would make fun of my Spanish. They didn't understand why I didn't speak it like everyone else. Mama told me she did it that way on purpose. She did her best not to speak it at home. She didn't want her children to suffer like she did the first time she came to this country, eleven-years-old in the second grade, and in all Special Ed. classes just because she didn't know English. She always felt like a second-class citizen because she was Mexican, a fruit picker. She wanted more for us. That's why my daddy is white. She told me I would do better because of it, as long as I never married Mexican. But I wasn't ever to tell, so I couldn't tell my cousins why—why I didn't speak Spanish with them, why there was never a way for me to fit in, how much they hurt me when they left me out and talked about my whiteness.

"No, but Rosa's granddaughter, she got the light eyes," Anita said. "She came out very pretty."

"Oh, I didn't know the daddy was white."

"He's not. He's Spaniard." Like somehow this was better.

I peeked out from behind the door, brave enough to throw mean faces when Mama shushed them after she had heard enough.

"*Mija* looks like my *suegra*," Mama said. "She's got her eyebrows." I thought about my white grandma and I was glad to have her eyebrows. They were very dark, slim and arched. They didn't have long spider legs reaching out over her glasses like Daddy's did. Mama always wanted to trim Daddy's brows, but he didn't let her. He said he liked them that way.

My older cousins, Anita and Soledad, rolled their hair in huge rollers and sprayed the Aqua Net again and again. Anita would be married soon and I thought if I could have just one wish, I would look like her and have big wide brown eyes and perfect teeth.

My *Tia* Lupe tried on Mama's new blouse. If it fit, she was going to keep it and *Tia* Carmen curled and recurled her eyelashes as my mother went through a box of clothes to see what else she could give away.

Grandma stayed in the kitchen with Maria, the oldest *tia*. She was nearly as old as Grandma and she didn't have teeth. Well, she had some, but they weren't in the right place or something. She had never married and she always had this look on her face like, "Where?" I liked her. She was always there and she didn't mind doing dishes. Together she and Grandma were perfecting the beans because everyone in the church, which meant everyone in the family, knew that Grandma's beans were the best around.

My *Tio* Ramon was outside with my dad, looking at the rusted dead Chevy in the backyard. Without words, they could share the dream of what it would be like when the car was painted and running. Without words, they could stand there and become better friends poking at a dead car.

I knew Daddy would be tired when this was all over and the *familia* had gone home. It had been a long weekend for him with people sleeping wall to wall in the living room and no place for him to escape. He had slept in our car the night before. He said it was so he could listen to the game and he just fell asleep, which could be true. Sometimes he did that, but it could also have been that he was getting a little tired of the people and constant Spanish chatter. He looked happy today, his blue eyes laughing when he joked, and the spider brows teasing up and down. I think he was just anxious to get this whole church picnic thing over with so everybody could go home.

Finally, it seemed after forever, my *tias* and cousins and the food, everything and everybody, was ready to go. We only had to load it all up and take off. There were three cars going and we stood outside, everyone debating who was going with who and also who was taking what.

My father brought out the steaming cauldron of beans, the lid jumping around as much as the women.

"Now be careful. Wait, don't drop it!" Mama cried, carrying potholders and chasing him as if she could catch the pot herself, if he should drop it right there in the front yard.

A chorus of "*Ay, Dios*" sprang up from Grandma and Maria as my dad navigated through the rough grass and dirt, making his way to the car, everyone following.

Tia Lupe, in Mama's new blouse, wanted the beans to go with her. She had the girls to make sure they wouldn't spill. But *Tia* Carmen wanted to take the pot with her because she was carrying Grandma, and she didn't want Grandma to worry about the beans on the way to church.

It must have really meant something to show up at the picnic holding the beans. Everyone wanted to take them. As it turned out, since Daddy carried that huge pot outside, they were coming with us.

Everyone got in their cars and we left. We weren't even a block away before the beans started coming, dancing down the windshield in pinkish-brown rivulets, all down, like when Daddy took us through the carwash except this was different, not the soapy kind of streams. No.

The streams started out pinkish-brown and then came the pinto beans shimmying down the windshield. Some came down end-to-end and some slid down their backs.

"William! The beans!" Mama shrieked. "We left the beans on the roof of the car!" She fluttered her hands, panicking.

Daddy kept right on going ignoring her with that tilt of his big wide chin and his wobble head. He was grinning, evil Grinch style. He wasn't going to stop. I knew that look which meant all bad things so I slid over to the other side, behind him where he might not notice me. He kept on driving real slo-ow, bean juice sloshing down side windows now, with beans jumping off everywhere in little bursts like his pent-up irritation. He put on the windshield wipers to clear them away, as if they weren't really there, and it was just rain or something. But the beans kept on coming, dancing, shimmying, sliding, some sticking to the wipers in little bean chunks while I tried to keep as quiet as possible and worried for Mama because she was not.

Mama cried and waved helplessly, motioning that her family was behind us. They'd worked so hard. Her mother's beans. Please, please stop the car.

The more upset she got, the more Daddy drove. He made it like a test for her to see when she would stop crying about the beans. I prayed for

Mama to please be quiet so everything would be all right.

Finally she was, and the silence reminded me of that part right before Mama would put a big ladle of pintos in the fry pan. She held her breath scrunching her face because she knew what was going to happen as soon as the juice of the beans hit. I always stood behind her and held my breath too, waiting for the firecracker sizzle of grease splattering.

We drove like that for another block or so pretending bean juice and beans weren't raining down on our car. Finally, Daddy pulled over. He stopped right across from the McDonalds. I wanted to run across the street and stay there. I didn't want to go to the picnic anymore. I didn't want to see my favorite cousins or my friends or eat or anything. I really wanted to go to McDonald's now.

I couldn't do that, so I stayed in the car, looking out the back window. I watched as the others, my cousins, my *Tios*, Grandma, those people, they pulled over too. I thought maybe they would help Mama. I watched as everybody got out of their car and stood looking at us with blank expressions. Maybe just some big eyes. Everybody watched as Mama struggled with the heavy, hot pot of beans. She spilled some on her skirt struggling to get it in the car and put it on the floor between her legs. She took a breath like the burn of hot grease and said, "Okay. I'm ready."

We all watched and didn't say a word. No one came forward to lift the pot from her. No one said anything. I thought they might be laughing on the inside, especially the young ones who didn't know better, who weren't married yet. They only knew they'd better stay quiet.

I know that inside their own cars they got brave, and talked about my dad saying, "That William, he's crazy. What was she thinking marrying that *gringo*?" I could imagine Grandma looking sad, Maria wondering where, and my *tias* all brave enough when Daddy wasn't close enough to hear.

We arrived at the church, pinkish-brown bean juice dried to the windows, bean chunks on the windshield wipers, and a half a pot of beans. The others there laughed to hear of the misfortune, a big joke, how funny, what a story, knee slapping and "no me digas!" while we hugged and kissed, greeting one another.

My brown and browner cousins all together ran in a swarm, black braids whipping behind them. I didn't know how to break in.

"Get a plate! Get a plate!"

"Here, Teresa, *mija*, eat," my tia Jenni said handing me a plate of rice and beans. Across the benches, I watched my Mama smile, long red marks on her leg, the pink stain on her skirt outlined in brown on the edges. I held onto my plate, with my rolled up flour tortilla and tears—tears I could no longer hold back.

MERGING IDENTITIES

illustrations by Geeta Pattanaik

Chinese Pavilion

Shore Temple

Pondicherry

Chai Time

Banana Sellers

AN IMMIGRANT'S PERSPECTIVE

Poems and Illustrations by Deenaz P. Coachbuilder

The Village Gossip

Rainier Serenity. Washington State

Raging Roosters

Alki Sunset. West Seattle

VOICES OF HOME

by Deenaz P. Coachbuilder

The smell of sandalwood
bare hennaed feet
filtered sunlight spraying
dappled lacework
on shredded
sarovar leaves.

Parrots screech
a collective conversation
atop a canopy of banyan trees.

The sun slowly retires
into the warm dusky Indian Ocean.

I am home again
instantly
time and distance crushed
longingly
within my fist.

Such an idyllic scene
pages from a travel brochure
old frustrations forgotten
tediousness and deadly ennui.

Only the voices
from the past
calling, calling
call.

THE GREEN HEDGE

by Deenaz P. Coachbuilder

Far from above, none of the sounds
of Mumbai city can be heard.
The setting sun drenches the tips
of balconied skyscrapers.
In the distance, crowded streets
border the landscape.
The dome of a mosque pierces the sun.

Through the glaze of dust and heat,
a quiet emerald oasis ascends.
Nine palms fringe an oval green lawn,
a cool breeze turns over the leaves
to their dark undersides,
while gulmohor boughs dally together
as they sway.

Here children chase each other,
shod in muddied designer shoes
across the manicured terrace
while maids watch hide-and-seek.
Pedigreed playmates barter video games
amid the scrap of roll and tease,
and scattered nursery rhymes,
as they bask in secure childhood.

From behind a green hedge
dark eyes watch the games.
Her only dress scarcely covers scarred knees.
Scabbed fingers tap longingly
in time with the infectious jingle of pop tunes.
Every day she sits on the outer side
of a gossamer hedge.

Spawn of an unschooled
vagrant woman who haunts
the crowded corner traffic stop
for spare change from captive cars,
she escapes each evening to
crouch down beside the emerald hedge.
She tells herself she doesn't care
when they don't call her to play.

In my fitful dreams tomorrow's fantasy
hovers quietly beside her,
where her shouts and laughter
might merge with theirs
in a swirling whirl of happy cries
as quivering rainbows twine through their hair.

SOMETHING GLISTENED

by Deenaz P. Coachbuilder

something glistened
in the early light

she looked
just as majestic as before

her crown
made jagged
in the struggle for freedom

her torch
the world's beacon

the eternal flame
of blinding beauty
bestowing enlightenment
to all

her flowing gown
a welcoming river
to the downtrodden

'tis nothing,
just the tears
on lady liberty's face.

On January 28th. 2017, President Trump's executive order closed America's borders to refugees and immigrants from seven Muslim-majority countries.

SKIN DEEP

by Deenaz P. Coachbuilder

"You are becoming as brown as a berry", my mother would say with concern, for we all presumed that Indian men preferred light skinned women. I would traverse the tree lined avenues of Mumabi, India, with my friends, stopping at sidewalk cafes and eating street food cooked off the pavement, then fresh coconut water with its skimmed creamy insides, and often a stop at our favorite shop for sweet cold paan[1].

My college friends were Hindus and Muslims, Parsis, Sikhs, Christians and Jews, from North Indian Kashmir and Delhi, to South Indian Tamil Nadu and the coasts of Kerala and Andhra. They were burnt umber beautiful from the south, and green-grey eyed Kashmiri sirens from the plains and plateaus of the Himalayas. Differences of religion, community and skin color unnoticed, we mingled, dreamed and schemed together, believing that we would conquer the evolving years.

My son, relatively fair of complexion, met, wooed and married a beautiful African American. After hours of a difficult labor during which I heard the heartbeat of this reluctant being-to-be magnified in the delivery room monitor, who worried about what our grandson would look like? We just wanted a healthy baby.

And there he was, a perfectly formed angel, soft wavy hair, skin as pink as pale rose petals, the edges of his ears and feet multicolored with little dark patches. An artistic sculpture rather than a living thing.

Over the months his coloring changed, like the unfolding stages of a painting, not pink anymore but a delightful creamy complexion, matching the darker coloring of his infant ears and feet. Those wavy locks, though still soft to the touch like the kiss of fine mist, have turned into lush tight ringlets.

I, who had never noticed skin color, am captivated with this changeling.

Only his eyes remain the same. Dark brown, intelligent, wary, sensitive.

[1] Paan- a preparation combining betel leaf with areca nut, a mouth freshener

REMEMBRANCE IN PHOTOGRAPHS

by Deenaz P. Coachbuilder

I unpacked them from the box in which they had been stored,
each photograph carefully wrapped in layers of newspaper,
forgotten in a darkened room which nobody visits.

Sepia and black, legends of a vanished epoch circle around
and ensnare me. Overlapping waves of dearly loved faces,
old fashioned saris and broad silk ties. My grand mother's favorite
perfume of lavender streams through my hair, the musty scent
of camphor in which they packed their treasures, all
tumble into my lap like suppressed shimmering memories.

Reflected in grand father's eyes are young cousins who climb trees
and throw down at passers by the pits of jambur fruit,
a wide gem-like lawn jealously sneaks its way between
posed bodies and a cuddly hyperactive black spaniel
while the Matheran[1] mountains sing their summer songs.

Listen. I hear their voices, they are not gone,
but hunt for a new world in mine.

---

[1] *Matheran is a resort in the western mountains of India*

LOVE AND HATE ON A FATEFUL 2017 FEBRUARY EVENING

by Deenaz P. Coachbuilder

two Indian men
in their thirties
both engineers
met after work for a beer
at a strip mall
in Austen's Bar and Grill
where they were well known

a man walked in
accosted the two friends
"get out of my country"
the T V was loud
they ignored him

but
he was back with a gun

shots rang out

one immigrant, Srinivasn,
a Hindu
was on the floor
dead
the other wounded

Brad removed his shirt
and tied it tight around Alok's
leg to staunch the bleeding
Ian was shot
trying to intervene

a few days later, Srinivasan's wife
Sunaya said they
had so many dreams…
they love America and wanted to
do much for "this" country
her heart broken

now he is every where
 and no where
his clothes
his side of the sink
she thinks of the way
he used to brush, shower
he was a very loved child
his father's
trusted son
she said
  as her voice
faded
  into
  a whisper.

On Feb.24th. 2017, in Olathe, Kansas, two legal Indian immigrants were shot by a Caucasian man who hurled racial insults at them. Srinivas Kuchibhotla, 32, died, while Alok Madasani, 32, was hospitalized.

HOPE

by Deenaz P. Coachbuilder

the eternal mystery,
the perfume of lavender
that lingers
after the flower has faded,
an embryo
that transforms into
womanhood holding
    the seed in her palms,
the yearning for a better something,
many things,
    anything.

It is about the edge of the world
where the precipice
                    drops
only
    to be able to float beyond the horizon
when the band stops playing
    and the bright lights extinguish,
the freedom of forgetting
even one's own name.

Hope is an uncluttered universe
where construct merges into abstract,
the desire to shed
the archeology of the past

while preserving the best of what we were,
with all creation owning
  the right to flourish,
for every birth is mine
  every death is mine.

Hope is the last second of waking
when one knows there may be
   no awakening.
It is a longing for a world
beyond this world
inhabited by the welcoming spirits
of the beloved
   in another eternity.

Commemorating the death of 49 precious individuals at an Orlando nightclub on June 21st. 2016

ANOTHER SOLDIER

by Deenaz P. Coachbuilder

ah lady Syria
you opened
your hand
and let slide
through
your
tapered fingers
one of my
sons
assisting
militia fighters
trying to oust
hate filled
warriors
bent
on shredding
your
ancient country

would that you
had curled
your fingers
ever so slightly
and sheltered
him from that
explosion

the day of thanksgiving

the day after
we cannot
touch
the leftovers

flowers
left
over
the funeral pyre
of
our heart

A decorated American Soldier died of his wounds from an improvised explosive devise in Northern Syria on Thanksgiving, 2016

A TIME FOR EUCALYPTUS

by Deenaz P. Coachbuilder

It is my birthday today.
"Just a small gift, Mother."
I unwrap a silver-green package.
Lotions to pamper me await my touch.
I lift the lid, the perfume of eucalyptus
rises from the mist of childhood.

With head mildly throbbing,
strained breath, watery eyes,
a fitful child's limbs move restlessly,
waiting for relief. The clock's pendulum slowly
drags before each click. The hushed house waits.

Suddenly, the front door sweeps open.
The house quivers and awakens.
A sari clad figure enters my room.
Mother kisses me. Vibrations of love and energy
encircle me. Stooping, she applies two small drops
of eucalyptus oil upon my pillow.
Breathing deeply, my eyes turn heavy
in contentment.

Now, naked pink trunked eucalyptus trees
hidden among showers of pale leaves
line the banks of Riverside lanes.
I shiver in remembrance when

their soothing perfume surrounds me
at the break of rain after a burning dry spell.

She carries this legacy of eucalyptus from
half a world away, my mother,
across the generations,
                in the mists of memory,
to my son.

Dedicated to my son Shahrukh

IN EVERY WAY THE WRONG ONE

by Angelica Maria Barraza

My father never read a book in his life
He said, you spend too much time worrying over something that will never love you back
He came to the states when he was a boy, 9 maybe, and slept on his brother's floor
It was before Orange County became an artery of Jalisco's longing
Before he fucked one too many putas and mom left him for a financial aid specialist
Before the world touched him, the bottle and God
Before he naturalized, filed bankruptcy and stopped showing up for custody hearings
Before he moved in with Mago in Lake Elsinore where he traded rent for manual labor
Pulling a lawn mower across the parched earth, sweating through muscle tees
The sun bronzing the stripe of his neck

Songs sobbing from the radio propped on a plastic chair
I was in every way the wrong one
With my crop tops and gringa shoes, pretending I could only hear English
My eyes brimmed with whitewashed families on TV
And I thought if I tried hard enough I could will away the hair from my upper lip
That I could read myself into the life of the fictitious girl who on page 12 is described as a sunflower
Leaning into mid-day light

And now, so many years have shed from the lining of our hungers
He and his new woman in a trailer off the 15 highway
Pushing 20 dollars into my hand when I come to visit from the university
These moments of atonement are their own kind of migration
Their own kind of sob, or dream or dismissal
Recently, we have taken to calling one another at night and making sense of the stars

THE GREAT EMPIRE OF ASSIMI-LANDIA

by Jose Luis Lopez, Jr

I am from leftover frijoles in a repurposed country crock butter container.
From the house with the ferocious tan lions in front.
I am from the prickly nopal that is stuck on my forehead.
I am from KLOVE blasting from the radio early Saturday mornings.
I am from Chespirito reruns and Chente rancheras.
I am from Southeast LA, where everyone knew that "vapporu", 7up, and Caldo cured all. Where my culture did not need to be explained.
Until I was unrooted and rerouted
To this Inland place where I found no Empire
This place, where my parents tried to find sanctuary
Really felt like purgatory.
I'm stuck.
My dark skin, my cultura stands out even amongst the Pochos who look like me. I'm now from a place where I have to prove my Americanism.
I am from assimilation and acculturation....get in where you fit in.
Until....
A teacher tried to call me "Joe"
Then I felt the blood of my indigenous ancestors
"Yo soy, Jose. Perdido en un mundo de confusion."
I am Jose, who like the Joaquin that Corky wrote about is "lost in a world of confusion,

caught up in the whirl of a gringo society,
confused by the rules, scorned by attitudes,
suppressed by manipulation, and destroyed by modern society."[1]
I am from here and there.
Bakers and King Taco
Dearden's and Living Spaces
Los Tigres del Norte and Tupac

And while el anaranjado and the self-appointed Captain Americas try to displace me and mine through deportation, incarceration, and gentrification in the hopes of making "Their America" great again.

I will remain here, eating frijoles from a repurposed Country Crock butter container in the Great Empire of Assimi-landia.

[1] *From "I am Joaquin" by Rodolfo Corky Gonzales, 1969.*

A SHORT GUIDE TO FINDING YOUR FIRST HOME IN THE UNITED STATES

by Minerva Canto

First, remember what your life was like before you and your family lived in a two-car garage. You were six years old and newly arrived from Mexico City. Santa Ana was a small city and you wondered why there were hardly any people walking on the streets. Few of them looked like you, even less spoke Spanish. How would you ever fit in?

You were grateful that Tia Maria and her husband were willing to share their one-bedroom apartment on Olive Street with you, your nine-year-old sister, Mamá and Papá. Never mind that Tia Maria and her husband enjoyed entertaining their friends almost daily, eating taquitos or other Mexican appetizers as they downed Coors beers until the skies were dark for several hours. If you timed it just right, you and your sister were able to finish your homework by sunlight while sitting on the wooden blue steps that led to the second-floor apartment. It wasn't the most graceful thing to do, balancing your notebook on one knee and textbook on the other, but you knew, already, school was one of the few good things in your life and you didn't want to mess it up.

It doesn't take Mamá long to figure out there's another possibility. The garage below the apartment is empty, has been for the few months you've been living in Southern California. One day, Mamá goes inside and sees that the owners have begun converting the garage into another apartment. It's sectioned off in two: one small room containing a full-size bed with a dingy mattress infested with cockroaches, and another, smaller room that contains a refrigerator, stove and dinette set with green chairs that remind you of guacamole. A small bathroom is off to the side. Yes, everything you need is there.

"She'll never rent the garage to you," Refugio tells Mamá. "Not in a million years." Tia Maria's husband is a tall, dour man whose eyes seem to disappear behind lashless sockets.

Mamá, who's grown up without a mother or a father, doesn't need anybody to tell her what to do. She thinks about what she will say as she waits for the owner to make her monthly visit to the apartment to collect the rent. As soon as Esther walks out the door, Mama rushes after her down the stairs.

"Esther! Esther! I need to ask you something."

Esther stops and waits.

"Would you be willing to rent the garage for us to live in?"

Mamá has already figured out a budget and offers to pay $100 in monthly rent. Esther won't have to do anything to fix it up; Mamá and Papá will make it habitable. Esther hesitates for a few moments, then agrees to Mamá's proposal.

Just like that, you have a new home of your own! Garage living, it's a dream come true. You are no longer los arrimados, forced to rely on others for a place to sleep. You almost forget that the garage doesn't have any drywall or insulation. Or that cockroaches and a few mice have already taken up residence. Or that the kitchen has no sink. Even you, at six years old, can wash dishes in the bathroom sink by standing on a stepstool.

As Mamá cleans the shower stall free of dirt, Papá nails long black sheets of rubber roofing material onto the inside of the large garage door to try to insulate the small bedroom against temperatures that sometimes drop into the 40s at night. They don't have money for drywall, so most of the walls remain bare, revealing the unfinished wooden studs.

With Mamá's first paycheck as a seamstress at a swimsuit factory, the family makes the first big U.S. purchase.

"My girls will have new beds," Mamá says.

The wooden bunk beds stand proudly next to the full-size bed, which Papá has sprayed with DDT insecticide. The chemical has just been banned as a pesticide on crops because it may cause cancer, but Mamá and Papá don't know this. DDT is the best way to evict las cucarachas from the stained mattress so that your parents can sleep on it after covering it with two comforters and a set of sheets.

You don't like it, but you begin to get used to the idea that you live in a garage. Mamá has been a seamstress most of her life and once dreamt of designing clothes for a fashion house. Now, she sews new curtains for the lone window in the garage, livening up your tiny kitchen and eating nook. She collects colorful cloth scraps from the trash bin at the swimsuit factory, until she has enough to sew into strips, which she then sews into patchwork quilts for all your beds.

You're embarrassed sometimes to tell other kids where you live, afraid they will anoint you "Garage Kid." Most residents in the neighborhood near downtown Santa Ana are working-class people living in modest, one story homes adorned with thick leafy trees. Most are Spanish-speaking Latinos, which means that most neighbors knew each other and parents take turns checking on children playing outdoors. Sometimes, you're playing outside and see Albert, the only white kid on the block, come out of his house across the street. He's around your age but he rarely plays with the other kids.

"Albert! Get back in here!" his mother's hoarse voice carries out her house and across the street. Often, you see the ruddy-faced woman yanking Albert around by the arm or ear. You hear your parents gossip that she is a borracha, too bad her kid has to suffer her drunken bouts. You decide that there are worse things than living in a garage.

There are lots of other kids in the neighborhood. Your sister finds friends easily, as always. Thin and lanky, with long limbs, she's a natural at climbing trees and jungle gyms. You're a shy kid who prefers staying indoors to read or play dolls. Your only neighborhood friend, Leti, loves dolls as much as you do.

One afternoon, you're sitting on the curb waiting for Leti to finish eating dinner when your sister comes running over to you.

"Come play with us," she says.

She and and a group of kids want to play kickball, but they need one more person for each team to have an equal number of players.

"Please," she pleads. "Only until Leti comes outside."

A book in one hand and a doll in another, you want to say, "No, I don't want to." But you love your sister and want to please her. She brushes your hair and pours your cereal each morning since Mamá and Papá leave for their jobs so early in the morning.

"You don't have to finish the game."

You reluctantly agree. Leti shouldn't be long now, you say to yourself as you leave your spot on the curb to join the team.

Usually, you play in the neighbor's front yard, a sprawling expanse of green surrounding the corner house. Today, that lawn is surrounded by low-lying white twine held up by wooden stakes, meant to protect newly installed sod. The neighbors think the twine is enough to keep kids away, but they're mistaken. The outfield team takes their assigned spots, everybody's sneakers casting deep dents in the soft green carpet.

You're up first. You stand at attention and wait for the ball, then you kick it with all your might and run as fast as you can toward first base. As you do, you trip on the twine and your forehead hits the faded red cement step leading to the neighbor's front door. You will remember the exact shade of red on that step long after that house has been demolished to make way for senior apartments. You will, thankfully, forget what it feels for your head to crack open on the edge of that step. You'll hear screaming, then your sister's voice as she gently turns you over. More screaming.

"So much blood!" your sister exclaims.

No one runs to get your parents. Instead, your sister puts one hand under your neck and another under your head as Maria, her best friend, puts her arms under your legs. They are ten years old, their bodies not much bigger than yours, but they feel the weight of responsibility more than the weight of your body.

"Perdóname! Perdóname!" your sister says, apologizing over and over through her tears.

Together, they lift you up from the ground and carry you next door, where you live.

At home, they place you on your parents' bed. Mamá and Papá run back and forth from the bedroom to the bathroom, collecting first-aid supplies. First, they must clean the wound and stop the bleeding. A flap of skin reveals a triangular shaped gash on your forehead, leaving for all to see a small portion of your skull. Papá doctors the cut, trimming along a strip of medical tape to create several butterfly bandages. The technique, used to temporarily seal a wound that requires stitches, is one he's learned during his years in the Mexican Air Force. Even as he's careful with the bandaging, Papá's mind races ahead to the inevitability of a hospital visit. He debates with your mom whether they should call an ambulance or a cab.

"An ambulance would be quicker and we don't know how serious the injury is. She could have internal injuries," Mamá argues.

"But if we call an ambulance, we'll have to answer a lot of questions," Papá responds. "No, no, we need to call a taxi."

The unsaid is left hanging in the air, a secret too dangerous to say out loud now or in future years, when your parents will have other tough decisions to make. It's clear that you have something else to worry about, something so major that Mamá and Papá decide they're willing to take the chance that you're stable enough to be transported in the back seat of a cab. Your sister remains by your side the entire time, holding your hand.

The cab arrives quickly and soon you're on your way to Tustin Medical Center. At the emergency entrance, Papá asks the taxi driver for the fare total. The taxi driver shakes his head.

"No charge," he says.

It's a kindness you will talk about for years to come, one you will repay to others who need it.

Once inside the hospital, you're assigned a cot in the patient area and a doctor arrives to examine your wound.

"Oh, that's a really good job!" the doctor says. "Who did this? Where did you learn such good bandaging skills?"

Papá smiles for the first time in hours. In all, the cut requires 11 stitches, but the doctor's praise seems to be the pronouncement your family needs to close the evening with relief. The good news is that you don't have internal injuries and your legal situation has not been uncovered in the ensuing chaos.

As the days pass, you become aware that your life isn't the norm. It's not just that you live in a garage. You've managed to advance past English-as-a-Second-Language classes after just one year in the United States, thanks to spending hours in the library and at home reading books. Being in a mainstream classroom, you see how different your life as a newly arrived immigrant is from kids who were born in the United States. The easy way they speak English, so self-confident that they aren't mispronouncing any words. Their families, who all speak English flawlessly. About one in four Santa Ana residents are Latino; seventy percent are white. The division between those who speak English fluently and those who don't is clear. Those who don't are teased about their immigration status and called "wabs," short for "wetbacks." The derogatory term refers to people who've come to the United States by swimming across the Rio Grande. You become determined to fit in, to become like everyone else, best to hide any evidence that shows otherwise. This seems the only recipe for success.

After your accident playing kickball, you become obsessed with the way your face looks. The bandages on your forehead set you apart from everyone else, even other immigrant kids. You don't like it when other kids stare at you.

One blustery February day, the bandages and stitches are finally scheduled to come off. Light raindrops wash the streets clean as you and Mamá take the bus, then walk from the bus stop to the hospital. Mamá's taken a rare morning off from work and you're absent from school. Everything seems to look brighter after the rain, making you giddy with anticipation. You almost don't mind as the doctor tugs on your forehead as he removes each stitch, one by one. You try not to squirm, anticipating the joy of having once more a face no one notices.

Finally, all the stitches are off.

"Please, I want to see," you tell Mamá.

She doesn't want to show you, but you insist. With small mirror finally in hand, you look at your forehead and are horrified to discover that tiny black train tracks run along part of your forehead. It's the 1970s and the surgical string does not yet dissolve by itself. The bruising hasn't completely healed and tiny bits of dried blood remain.

There's no way around it: your face looks like a mess. You're young, still in second grade. Though you're already reading at third grade level, you think your face will forever look monstrous. No, that isn't too harsh a word for what your forehead looks like right now. Even Frankenstein had stitches running down his forehead. Who's to say that the image in the mirror won't always look like that? Mamá tries to reassure you, telling you that further healing will take place in the coming days. Sure, the doctor says the same thing, but you're an immigrant kid. You've known your share of disappointments and have no reason to believe you've seen the last of them. You cry uncontrollably and beg to go home for the rest of the day.

"Mamá, I can't go to school looking like this!"

But she needs to take you to school immediately so she can go work the rest of her shift at the sewing factory. You don't have a choice, but do get Mamá to agree that you can wear your knit hat all day so your forehead can stay covered.

You are learning, little by little, what parts of yourself are safe to reveal.

AN *HIJO* OF IMMIGRANTS

by Anthony Victoria

Part I: The Beginning

Ni de aquí, ni de allá. 'Neither from here or there' in English—the words succinctly serve as a constant reminder of my Honduran-Mexican-American ethnicity. In the span of 26 years I have endured the hardships many Latinos confront in the United States. I have been called a 'wetback' and 'spic'; I have been told by teachers and so-called mentors that my destiny was only to work or go to prison. And yet, despite those experiences, I realize it compares little to the struggles of my parents—immigrants who left their barrio and pueblo to pursue the American Dream.

My *mamá*, a strong and proud woman, left behind her two eldest children to find better work up north. Tela Atlantida, Honduras is a tropical kingdom—full of palm trees, banana plantations, and exotic species. However, this is merely a visual distraction that belies the political corruption and gruesome violence that continues to plague my mother's *paisanos*. Feeling trapped by her former, cowardly partner—a man she said verbally and physically abused her—she made a tough decision. Leaving behind 3-year-old and 2-year-old boys pained her deeply. They would spend their early years without her—finding no comfort from their drunkard father and left with gnawing abandonment. It is a deep scar that affects *mamá* to this day. My *abuelito* (grandpa) Don Luis Midence, a former labor organizer that fought tooth-to-tooth against the United Fruit Company, once told my *mamá:* "You're only going up there to be treated like a second-class citizen. That's how they treat people like you and I—like we're nothing. Might as well stay here."

My *papá*, a timid, yet hard working man, spent his youth frolicking the highlands of Tepexco Puebla, Mexico. I remember hearing as a kid the stories of my dad walking to school barefoot or with my *bisabuela's* (great-grandmother's) sandals. Despite the laughing howls of his peers, my papá said he stood tall and walked tall. It was a principle he learned from his great-grandfather. As a Nahuatl descendant, Don Andrés learned to live in humility, while also appreciating the grandeur of the indigenous lands. My paternal great-grandfather didn't care about materialism, or fitting in. His focus was catering to the land and he taught his grandson the same. And yet, although he will not admit it, my father lacks the assertiveness of a proud man. This I understand. His father, my *abuelo*, was killed in an accident in Veracruz when he was three months old; my *abuela* decided to leave my father in the hands of my *bisabuelitos*, leaving to Morelos to start a new family. It may be the reason why he's acted cold heartedly with his own family and why he struggles to grasp the importance of providing comfort. As painful as it is, I empathize with my father.

Both my mother and father crossed paths in the mid-1980s. Ronald Reagan was U.S. president at the time, the Cold War was at its climax, and the economy was teetering towards crisis. They were both working inside the heat-congested sweatshops of the San Gabriel Valley sewing cheap fabric for menial pay. It was then that the petite, light-skinned woman from Tela would meet the thin, tall and dark Mexican man from Tepexco. They didn't know it, but our Victoria-Midence legacy in the United States was born right then and there. Both of them have never really spoken in depth about why they decided to date. If I were to infer, I would say it is because they recognized each other's strengths. My *mamá* recognized my *papá's* dedication to work; my *papá* recognized my *mamá*'s *loyalty*. In their logical minds these two traits would combine to build a strong foundation. And this is fair thinking; in a nation such as the United States a family nucleus needs stability to endure trials and tribulations. However, as with many immigrant families that are embroiled with paying the price of being 'model citizens', they did not have the time to love.

This played a role in their road to becoming U.S. citizens. After receiving amnesty through Ronald Reagan's Immigration Reform and Control Act of 1986, my *papá* with the help of my *mamá,* saved enough money to move from a small, cramped garage in La Puente, California to a tolerable apartment in nearby Pomona. Some would say living in the projects of 'P-Town' in the late 1980s and early 1990s was unbearable. For them, this was the beginning. Ten years after my father and mother met inside a *maquiladora* (sweatshop) in the City of Industry, *papá* took the oath that made him a naturalized citizen. It was an arduous road that forced him to risk life and limb—and yet it was a proud moment. My *mamá* would wait seven more years to receive her moment of truth, but it would be the same fulfillment my *papá* felt before her. The two 'hat-in-hand' undocumented immigrants earned their right to be here. No one could ever take it away from them. However, they knew and understood that their naturalization came at a heavy cost.

LOS FELIZ ON THE SLY, AVERY SCHREIBER IN HIS BLUE ROLLS, TINKER TOYS IN THE GUTTER, FOAMY BANDANA IN A GUCCI BAG

by Linda Ravenswood

When i was a little girl
living in perfect, broken,
golden, *netsuke* barbie dreamhome
with erratic, mayflower, perfection mama
and first husband —
poor immigrant 'dirty NDN' father —
then refugee israeli second husband
(or them in-betweens
we aren't supposed to talk about
go back to bed, linda)
teevee was heav'n on earth—
    and there was a thread //
    a recurring image //
every woman's face
(after about) the third set of commercials
was blown up

to reveal
a robot underneath—
    how pretty she was
    before the deluge //
her smile and bonnie bell lip stick //
her breck smooth'd hair
and cream colour'd cowl neck //
a vittorio gassman-cum-jordache
bistro gardens-robert culp-*fruszen gladje*
kind of thing // and then
boom // her face blows up
right before the end card.
    those mechanised eyeballs
    those wick wires
    and lip service
    on the fritz

goodbye corey good bye corey good bye corey

pretty lady
so
pretty pretty pretty

SELF-ACKNOWLEDGED CHOLAS I LOVE

by Linda Ravenswood

Revekka —
'My grand father
was born in 1920
and he always smelled of tobacco
so strongly
and Tres Florés
slapped
on both sides
of his face.'

Silvy —
'We are empowering ourselves
when we make our own work.
We are empowering ourselves
when we show our work in public—
plainly, truly.
When we do that
we empower and inspire other people,
especially girls,
to make work
and tell their story.'

Cintia —
'She look'd like Sandra Medina,

eyes the same green / brown
as her hair / a florid earthy color
where leaves and dirt mingle.
On her face
the shade
made her glow
all red / all yellow
like fruit skin in summer.'

Stella —
'I went to NYC
and got so much attention
which is crazy, because
in L.A. they got no love
for my wide hips and big ass.
But in Bushwick,
they loved me
because the only Mexicans in New York
are from Pueblo
and it's like, one guy
and one girl
brought their whole families over,
so every Mexican in NYC
looks Mayan
with real
Cara de los Indigenos.
You can always
spot them
keeping to themselves
and marrying each other
to maintain that Pueblito look.
In Bushwick, its lots of Centro Americanos
y Cubanos, Puerto Ricans and Dominicans
even South Americans

but very few Mexicans, you know.
The Dominicans and Puerto Ricans
loved me there.
They said, 'Ay, what are you?'
And I said, 'I'm Mexican, guy!'
And they said 'Ay, no you're not —
Mexicans are petite y Indio'
And I was like
'Dang, I'm Mexican though'
and we laughed.
Then finally, one day
this guy who'd been out to L.A.
saw me; I was painting faces
for extra money
and he came up
on the street
with his finger wagging
and said 'I know what you are!
You're a Chola!'
And that was amazing,
because unless you've been to L.A.
you really don't understand
what it is to be Chicana.'

LITTLE ARMENIA

by Linda Ravenswood

When I was growing up
across smooth balcony
back behind black wrought-iron
Angie knelt, Angie Survivor
of Armenian Genocide.
When I knew her
she was in her seventies,
her house a Shangri-la
next to my grandmother's walkup—
two paradise apartments
beside each other —
one from the east
with western touches
and one from the west
with the Byzantine edge
all antique rooms lean to.
How many high puddings did she make ?
How many dimes did she slide
in the Easter pie for me to find ?
Such sweet songs and stories
of walking Constantinople
blessing her memory
remembering her crossing
nursing in Chicago
watching a century take flight—

Angie, stitches sewn,
under warm fingers
and pearls, Angie
soft garments to weave.
There is no marker
for Angel Vahan Moomjian
who danced this planet
a hundred and four years.
When she died
she donated her body to science.
In visions, Angie stands,
her fingers plunging
a basket of orange lentils
in the open market
showing me deep
bright treasures of earth.

THE SAINT

by Linda Ravenswood

My aunt and uncle come from La Paz.
They infuse the house with Spanish
and salted white cheese. They talk
new cars and the tranquility
of their home in the pueblito.
Their stories are Cabo Fiero
and slippery Uncle Pablo
who stole corn flour, sugar
and tequila for the poor —
how he spent decades
playing cards in the border town
running a hotel for prostitutes
he named for a saint. They show
a smudgy picture, Tio Nicolas
in crossed *bandolieros,*
his chest a battered map
in multi crease.
When the guitars come out
the uncles sing full throated
with a pride that touches terror.

My aunt and uncle come from La Paz.
They talk of the horse culture on the *rancho,*
the beauty of ranch animals
riding saddle up against ocean.

They gawp the glistening boulevard
in Hollywood, fanning clean dollars
for *jugo de amanzano* from a *paletera.*
Things are familiar, but strained.
They already know prices are better downtown.
Their faces clamber in window displays
burning Hidalgo, Sanchez Taboada,
Chuahoctemoc, stone stares
from the *Paseo de Los Heroes* in Tijuana.
What do I know. Cars flash,
and we are legs out, walking through.
Chaos. They seem vulnerable, small
as memories in the crosswalk. Long
south is home in the Baja, that fingery
elision escaped from upper Califia. My uncle
says *this when you need a horse*
as he sidesteps the racket.
Vamos Princessa, he says.

On days when he would come—
with vegetables and cake,
dolls, and money for my grandmother—
my father would hoist me high
and say *Caballo* to my one Spanish ear.
The first word between us.
Caballo. A coincidence,
a genetic response? To a dark house
loaded with European antiques,
he would come and tell me things I forgot I knew.
Once he brought a white buffalo I could sit on.
Sturdy, a game. A guardian. A replacement.
Like the bison of the plains, it disappeared —
to spaces between dust motes
when the sun at five in the afternoon

smears such painful edge to light.
Things we pretend we own.
My grandmother sold the buffalo,
like a white woman would do,
to one of her customers,
as if the legacy of my father
and his gifts,
weren't mine—
neither to embrace
nor or to deny.
What does a child want a white buffalo for ?
What does she want with desert walkie talkies ?
Or a lariat ? Save it for later.
The ministry of her clever eyes!

My aunt and uncle wear shoes of hammered leather from Baja.
They come with minty dollars in *mitu* fingers.
They are other world in the sitting room—
They are proud, they say.
Ay, Linda, we the proud people;
but I think they are telling more stories.
I think they're stunned   at what the world
has made   of what   they believed
was beautiful   and important.   *Caballo.*

Who is the one who points to the sun?
Who is it who speaks—*Sun* ?
An artist perhaps—an ersatz pointer—
or a poet   one who cries Rain
never having seen it.
A poet is a sad bugger—
sad as a Mexican howling love songs
and waiting to be fed. *Pan tostado, mija.*
Mande. The Mexican must be

the most human of all —and
the Mexican singer,
the saddest evocateur
of some swatch of time
on earth.

COLD SONG IN A HOT CLIME

by Linda Ravenswood

56°F,
Wind, North,
3 miles an hour,
100% humidity,
Naperville, Illinois ...
the phone started ringing
a rolled over sound from long ago
I didn't recognize the number
but said 'Hello'
and a woman's voice
came back 'It's Sandy,
Sandra Bland.
I don't know you,
do you know me ?
My eyes are closed,
someone
gave me a phone
in the dark:
Are you white?'
Closing down the receiver
like an earphone
in a recording studio, I said,
'Mom? Is that you?'
'No, it's Sandy,
something happened.'

I put my face in the pillow,
Alice Coltrane eyes. Sometimes,
if you're lucky you can see rainbows there
and I said eyes tight,
whole face a crumpled
sheet of music, 'Sandy'?'
She said,'I know what happened.'
but I said, too fast
instead of listening,
'Where are you ?'
    'gone.'
There was a horrible
long silence,
soto voce, grey shocking
break in the coda,
and I opened my eyes
a quick second
to see if I was in my room /
still passing through / and not /
    false stop
    whip turn
    pull over
    put out
    your cigarette
/ you running blue black
in the daylight
where ever you are / strong /
strong running blue / black
strong running blue / black
strong running blueback / you / running high /
your fleur-de-lis in the cloud / you know /// your rights
    / don't say my name / don't know my name from this /
    stop saying the wrong name /

there's a job in Texas
'Sandy? you still there?' '
Mm hmm,' she said.
'Remember the time they tried to have a party but everybody got sick
and the party was called off? And remember when we got the offer from
Texas, nobody could ever hold a job like that, that job was a
fleur-de-lis in the clouds, something to make us go on and on and on,
HeathCliff and Cathy in the distance, something to make us believe in
love, all men ... '
and a high mountain gaida came screaming across the valley / a tar bleating on the breeze
can I hold your memory ?
Where did you go ?'
'Yeah but are you white?'
and the top note went across the staff of sky,
connecting one thing to another, linking hands,
genetic passageways, the deep sea,
I'm forever blowing bubbles, thread of eon,
my grandmother's watch and fob,
and Sandy said
'That's lucky'
And the receiver went cold,
and the song was over

100,000 BELLS OF MY HEART

by Linda Ravenswood

this is everything I know about the man on the train / he loves his family / it has cost him a lot of money to get this trip / he will be in Stockton on Saturday / he's calling everyone he knows / his *primos* / his *tias* / his friends / he keeps asking *is the truck okay / did you get the money / did you make money angel / angel did you make money on this run / meet me at the place in Stockton so we can change the trucks / Alicia is coming before June to get the truck / meet me there and bring that thing / you know what I'm talking about right* / he calls everyone / *tia / mija / mijita / primo* / because everyone is interchangeably / *tia / mija / mijita / primo* / because he is a mexican adult male / he tells them he took the children to the graves of their uncle and father / cleaned the graves *a little bit of someone's father* / says / *we'll be in town soon / have it ready* / he tells a woman he's going to be *in San Bernardino for 5 minutes / meet me on the platform so I can give you money for the children and kiss you* / this is everything I know about the man on the train / I haven't seen him but he must be wiry because he's such a stress case / he asks the family *are your phones working* / his calls keep getting dropped / it's vacation but he cannot stop // maybe he was talking to no one / maybe he has no plans / maybe he's alone as everyone else / this is everything I know about the man on the train

MACKEREL'S REVENGE

by Linda Ravenswood

I am the jew who can hold her breath longer than anyone.
I was born in *Saintes-Maries-de-la-Mer* where we lived
til the Boches tore in. They came, grey draped
with fabulous throats calling through the streets at dawn.
Metallic torsos slipped in and out between blinds in the evening
when the high beam would catch them on the lapel
or shoulder. Then again, maybe it was pure moonlight.
They said we'd been sitting long enough on our asses
praying, studying in our own language. They said
we never did a hands' turn for anyone except our own
the way we loaned out money and traded gold and diamonds
made them want to retch. They said they came to show us
the value of a more honest work. We shrugged
but they actually came through the door one evening.
By nightfall we stood / frozen meat in Polish mud.
They said we had to work but first they had to prepare us
so they shuttled us down a piece of gangway and said
shower up but it was all lies. The shower had no water
in the pipe / just a hissing odour of yellow almonds.
And Tanya said / *do the trick* so I crouched down
between vomiting ladies turning into each other
clutching / and I made my breath / the longest breath I ever did /
chin to chest / down to cement like I showed the kids in the village.
I went low as I could and held it deep / and there I saw
the ladies of the perimeter / the ones by the vent holes /
blood out of their ears and skin spotting pink.

And I tried to hold it / but I felt an agony under the skin
like air being sucked through pores / and there was little
use holding my famous breath. The almonds kept on
and there was no inch left to hide. And now, I am a fish.
I have *fishmind* but also the memory of sand / hot
on my once and forever limbs. If only
someone could slug me out of water to a big net
and sell me inland. I wouldn't mind the oven
or the sting of embarrassment anymore, so long as
any one of my slim bones could lodge in the gizzard
of a grown-up-child of a Nazi. Or an old Nazi dribbling
in a nursing gown. And I am scooped up !
The skiff pulling me in and I am gulping again—
again I try to hold my breath but the air is devastating
to my fisheyes / fishlungs. They tuck me in cottony ice. And
I can't believe the whole town didn't come out to line the road
in human chain / filling the street with songs of brotherhood
to stop them // They none of them got together and said
these are our neighbours, get the hell out of here
or we'll kick your ass back to Germany.
But now I have other business so I have to focus.
Ice covers me, more fish are coming. And
I remember looking down at my shoes,
the soft leather, and I said *what the f***ing hell* to no one,
but mother saw me and said *yes, but be a lady*
and they took us in a wagon and I am slipping —
I have to send the memory to my bones
to try to get to Germany to find someone
to pay back for all these lives.
I know I should be finished
and revenge is pointless. I'm trying.
But everywhere, everywhere,
there's Nazi's, and their children. And
they all love fish.

CROSSINGS

by Leticia Velasquez

I hear the whistle blow.

The Union Pacific freight train whistle still sounded in Corona early mornings before daybreak as the train travelled west. The streets hushed, the morning commute yet to begin, I can hear the lone sound from four miles away, faint and soft against the undisturbed quiet.

The train must be about to cross Sheridan Street, site of one of several crossings in Corona. When I was a child, the whistle signaled the time close to my grandfather's waking hour.

I, at this hour, am not awake. That is, I haven't risen from bed; I lie, eyes closed, moving in and out of sleep. I picture the crossing. When I see the crossing, it is always night. A night with sky not so blown out by big-city lights, sometimes dark and punctuated by starlight, other times filled with white cottony clouds hanging still.

When younger and out on teenage rambles with friends, we'd cross this way. On leaving Burr, we'd walk south along Buena Vista until it dead-ended onto Railroad where we'd make a right. In a few blocks, we'd turn south again, onto Sheridan, and walk another few miles to a friend's place.

The whistle blows again. Who else is listening? With whom am I sharing the sound across space? Who is awake? Who is going to work? Who is coming home?

My father, when he lived, would go to work at this hour, at a Chino dairy, to milk cows.

This hour is the only time of day that the whistle is audible from inside my childhood home. The whistle at this hour had always called my attention. Of course, I wouldn't always catch it, not if I happened to be sleeping deeply. When I did though, it was a welcomed familiar.

Though the sound doesn't uniquely belong to Corona, it's still one of the sounds from home, my childhood home. Sundays, daytime, while at the city park, where we'd go what seems to me like every Sunday, I'd hear the whistle. The loud whine would cut through the cacophony of different voices at the park and whatever traffic might have been moving along a small city's main street on a Sunday late morning or early afternoon, the park perhaps less than a quarter of a mile away from the tracks.

I hear the whistle again.

After an eleven-year leave, I'd returned to California.

*

My grandmother likes the violin. Or should I say fiddle? She let me know when I played *O Sister! The Women's Bluegrass Collection.* For the first time, she expressed a strong response to music, at least, it was the first time I heard her do so. For the first time, she expressed *her taste* for music; for the first time, she mentioned liking any of the English language music played in the house.

In Spanish:

"Are you playing this music?"

"Yes, why *ama*?"

"I'm just surprised."

"Why *ama*?"

"Because I like this music. It's music from my time. I like the violín."

I was doing laundry and I'd set up my mother's CD player/radio in the garage. I'd been playing the bluegrass CD on repeat since picking it up on a whim at the Folk Music Center in Claremont. Around the ninth or eleventh song, during "Blow, Big Wind" or "Coming Down From God", presumably after hearing the initial 15 or 20 second fiddle instrumental of the song, my grandmother finally stepped out from the kitchen to ask about the music.

It had never occurred to me that she had musical taste - that there was music my grandmother would pick out as *liking*, and even respond joyously to. I knew that my grandfather had liked *corridos*, but she?

In Mexico, they had listened to music at fiestas or in the streets, live music. *Banda* at the fiestas, serenades in the streets. Sometimes, musicians from other *pueblos* looking to earn some money would visit and play. And the *pueblo* had its own musicians—a few men. One, a violin player that sang.

Then there was the man in town who owned a generator that powered up a film projector. He'd play music. For the entire *pueblo*. By default. Speakers were set up outside and the music could be heard throughout the town. A song would be played on weekend days from the small theatre after announcing and before showing the featured film. And there was the *cantina*, where music also played. There, men sometimes paid for a serenade to someone not present. This music, too, heard throughout the town.

It is a small *pueblo*, with a population of about 3,000 and rural. Electricity wasn't installed until 1964, so listening to music prior to then hadn't been a private affair. (My grandfather, though, did return from one of his times as a bracero in the U.S. with a battery-powered radio. I'd have to ask my mother what they had been able to pick up on the radio.)

And so because of the above, coupled with my grandmother's lack of expressing her musical opinions, I had assumed that my grandmother had never acquired much interest in music, had never cultivated a musical taste. Actually, it hadn't been an assumption. It even hadn't been thought about.

How much of our music had she endured without complaining? Thinking in her own terms that it *sucked*. She'd never shown us her dislike. She'd never told us to play something else or to shut off the music. At least, not that I remember her doing so.

Maybe she hadn't minded some of the Spanish music that my older aunt and uncle played. And maybe she found softer sounds like those of Simon and Garfunkel, and maybe even oldies, tolerable.

But what about the disco? The funk? The James Brown or Rick James? The Jackson Five?

Or Kenny Rogers' "The Gambler?" My first music record, a birthday gift and so I had no part in the selection. Nevertheless, I played it constantly, danced to it, and learned the lyrics to "The Gambler." I was 10 years old and *Kenny Rogers* was the only music record that was *mine*. Maybe she liked the Kenny Rogers album.

That's another assumption, though. Why would Kenny Rogers be closer to *something Mexican*? What do I have in mind? *Rancheras*? I'd actually have to sit down and do a comparative listen between the two. Is there anything shared between Kenny Rogers and *rancheras*?

Wait, even if there is, why am I assuming that it is *rancheras* that would appeal to her?

*

The house now emptied of my aunts and uncles and my sister and me, only my mother and grandmother left, is mostly silent of ambient noise.

The ones responsible for the music in the house had been my aunts and uncles, and then my sister and I. Yes, my grandfather liked *corridos*, which I'd discovered when on a visit home I brought with me a tape with *El Corrido del Caballo Blanco*. He, though, never purchased records, tapes, eight-tracks. He might have never even entered a record store, not even a Spanish music one. If my grandmother listens to music, it's on her small AM/FM kitchen radio tuned to the local Catholic station. Same with my mother, I believe.

*

Instead of flowers for mother's day or a birthday, I think what they—my mother and grandmother - need at the house in Corona is a CD player and a music collection. I'd have to purchase the music. They don't shop at music stores. And it has to be a physical collection. They don't use the internet or computers.

Of course, I haven't asked if this is what they'd like. In defense of my assumption, I'm not thinking this is what they need because the silence needs to be filled. Not at all. It's just what I'd like to offer them as an exchange.

They give me the sounds of Spanish when I visit, something that I miss. It's here, in my childhood home, when visiting, that I most hear and use Spanish again. I won't write right now what that means to me, but I'll just say that it's *not* necessarily that the language constructs or structures my thinking differently, or makes me see the world differently. It's a complex of things, some the memory, some just, to my mind, the *physicality* of the language.

Perhaps I'm a keeper of sound.

I have the sound of a prayer call from my last two years in NY, in residential Brooklyn. It was the first time I'd heard a prayer call. At first I wasn't sure what I was hearing. I was outdoors, in the backyard area of my ground floor brownstone apartment. The call came from westward of me. I would only catch it when I was outside. It wasn't until after the second or third time that I recognized what it was.

Faint, soft, it also conjured its own image, carried its own sense of a history. This one, to my mind, ancient—at least as ancient as people alternately calling for mercy from and singing *alabanzas* to an unseen force. And because I couldn't see where the prayer call originated in Brooklyn, it was as if I was crossing with a place and time now only aurally extant.

IMAGES: WHERE HAVE ALL THE MEXICANS GONE

by Leticia Velasquez

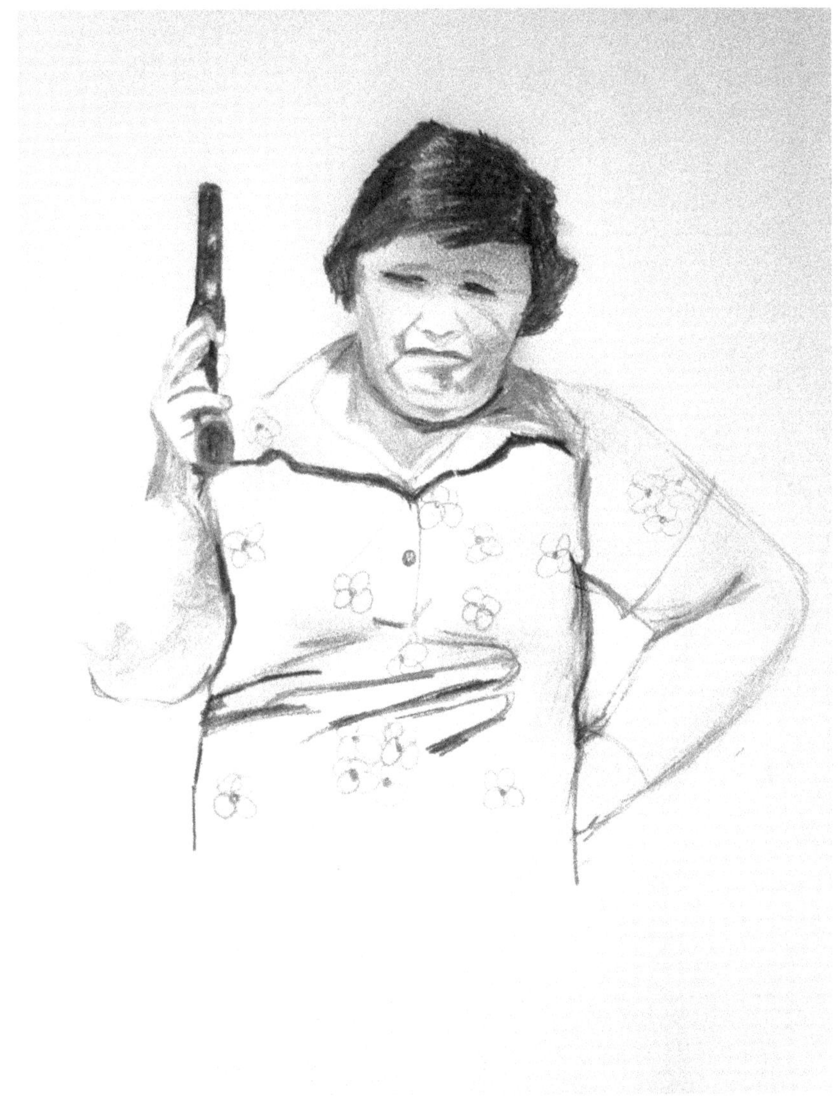

ABUELA

by Kimmery Moss

You died on April first,

the day I saw four old ladies
sipping tea from floral china
at a table near me
so near me
I was sure they heard me
whisper to a friend
I never really had grandparents

Really, none?

One grandfather, Miami, deceased
One grandmother, Ohio, deceased
Seen
a few days, a few times
One, never seen, deceased
long before me

I missed them though
I hardly knew them
Though
I know I am them

And you.
We didn't talk about you
but there must be you
in me too.

But how—
how
how will I recognize
someone I never really knew?

ABUELO

by Kimmery Moss

I watch them put you into a hole in the wall
next to your brother, Raphael.

Two men who look like us
mix plaster in a bucket and seal you inside.

It is sunny
on Rose Hill
where there are no roses.

I see my father's face—
He prays.

A man whom I do not know speaks loudly.
He celebrates you.
His words echo off the mausoleum floor
and off other people I do not know
but should.

I shiver.

The white marbled walls steal warmth—
I feel as cold as you
because we come together for funerals
and if we weren't family
we would be strangers.

I struggle to speak Spanish with them
like I did   in Miami   with you
while you sunk slowly into hospital sheets.

Eres muy bonita, mija
Blood tries to reenter my face but is stubborn
Gracias, I say

You visit me, this time
California
I'm supposed to say goodbye

Some words I am still learning:
Muerte
and *Abuelo.*

THE CALL

by Kimmery Moss

My father called me today
It was eight 'o six in the morning
but I noticed near noon.

Eyes roll back,
What happened now?
Suddenly weary
I dial, buttons punched hard

You called?
I did. How are you?
Well, and I meant it.
It was a sunny day.

I wanted to tell you
that my mother has died.

oh

I am sorry. I say.
Are you,   ok?

I am.

Breathing in, only in.
And it was peaceful?
A morphine drip,

An empty room,
An empty mind,
Yes.

I love you, Dad.
I love you too.
I just thought you should know.
Thank you.

Most people would cry
but I,
I was prepared for this.

I missed you long before you died,
Nostalgic
for nothing.
When your brain left you, he told me
When your heart left you, you showed me

Most people have names for their grandmother:
Mimi
Grammy
Abuela

You were Dora.
Always
The mother of Pedro,
never the grandmother of me.

You never knew
Me
Never tried

And yet—
I wondered if my kindergarten picture
was still next to your bed

An empty one now.

AMA-MY MOTHER

by Pati DeRobles

I write this as a cry for forgiveness, as an attempt at redemption for failing so miserably to be the daughter my mother deserved, to be the daughter I wish I had been. I write this as my love letter to my sweet angel mother, mi Ama.

But more than anything, I write this as a gift for my mother's family and especially for her grandchildren and great-grandchildren, that they may know the strength, the beauty, the love of their matriarch. May they know more of her life -her courage, kindness, and generosity and what losing her met to our family. That they may know the depth of their roots.

There are only a few events in life that each day you wake; you are struck by a sense of shock and terrible sadness by the realization that it wasn't a nightmare. That devastating, life-altering event really happened to you, in your very real life. Year after year, the shock begins to fade and the sadness remains as a close companion. Left no other choice, you make tenuous peace with the sadness and play along because you are reminded daily, life goes on, as it must.

On the day Ama died, March 7, 1984, she was a few weeks shy of 54 years old. At that age, she was already a grandmother to Luis, Gabriel, Juan, Karina, Hector, Gerardo, and David. Each grandchild, was her treasure and joy, and she loved and cared for them with a sweet tenderness. She had been raising Gabriel (her Pollito) as one of her very own. At the time, she was also caring for her maternal grandmother for some time. Abuelita Lucita Rivas was in her early nineties and had been living with us for quite some time after my mother brought her to Altadena from Mezquitic. She was also caring for our dear cousin Crisanto Gallegos, whose own mother had tragically passed away a few years prior. Our cousin Damian, who came to the U.S. to work, lived with us as well. When she died she was caring for a house that was home to at least 13 of her beloved: a backyard full of chickens, a couple of cats, dogs, parakeets, and her flourishing plants, trees, and flowers. Throughout her long days and in the evenings she sewed for hour upon hour to help support her household. When she died, I was 14, the twins were 12, Victor almost 16, Pancho 17, Goyo, Octavio and Tita in their early twenties and the eldest children, Miguel, Elsa, Zenorino, and Roque were just reaching their thirties Each making a life of their own, but always leaning close to our mother.

The very full house, bursting at the seams, the caring over so many, the animals, the garden, the sewing, and as incredible as this may sound, none of this was unusual -it was how she lived, all that she lived for and how she loved.

My memories of Ama are few but what remains is a clear understanding of her essence—who she was, as a person. In her essence, my mother was a most gentle, unassuming, yet courageous servant. I do not believe she ever thought to deny her help to anyone. If she could not help or offer her generosity, it pained her deeply and it was never of her own doing, or her own decision. Some of the memories that remain are related to this, her servant heart. Throughout the mid-seventies and into the early eighties, I remember multiple trips to Tijuana with a relative or another for one very specific purpose. Because we were so many children in our family, and because my father by virtue of having being born in the U.S., was able to naturalize most of his children born in Mexico (give us U.S. citizenship), my mother had in her possession 'papers.' 'Papers' meaning she had proof of U.S. citizenship for her many children of various ages that could be used for the service of others. My mother, to fulfill the desire (better said, the need) of many of her relatives and acquaintances' to bring their own Mexican-born children or other relatives into the U.S., used those 'papers' to do just that. Two or three of us kids would be her companions/decoys as another relative would drive us to Tijuana and we would return with one or two more kids (sometimes younger, sometimes older) to join their family in the U.S. Was this an illegal act? Of course it was. Was it an act of service and courage to actively defy laws and economic circumstances that serve to separate families? It most certainly was, but ultimately it was an act of love in the service of others.

In the thirteen years that my mother lived in the U.S., she never learned to speak English, she never learned to drive, and she got scared every time she stepped on to an escalator and though she was a petite, humble, quiet woman she was the most unafraid person, in the service of others.

With this memory, the devastating pain of her loss thoroughly breaks my heart, but my admiration and love for this sweet little courageous mother of mine grows and grows.

By 1976, after five years in the United States, my mother had 8 of her 12 younger children in public school. She had kids in at least four Pasadena schools from kindergarten up to high school. She could not help us with homework, talk to our teachers, visit the school, but I do not remember a morning when she would not gently wake us all up for school and rare the day we stayed home from school. If it was a cold morning, she'd tuck our clothes under us to warm them up before we had to put them on and sent all of us ready to school with a breakfast of warm avenita (oatmeal made with milk, sugar, and cinnamon) or a licuado (a shake made up of three ingredients; milk, an egg, and a banana). I had no way of appreciating at six years of age or even at fourteen years of age (the year she died) how she managed—each morning— to get as all off, on time, well fed and as ready as we could be, for school.

In the summer of 1983, the summer before she died, my mother took her last trip to her true home, her beloved Mexico. She brought my nephew Gabriel and I along with her as her companions. She loved going to Mexico and was most happy and relaxed there, though it was far from a leisure vacation. Upon arrival, she was a woman on a mission. Her first mission was to visit and sit with every relative, every close friend, and old neighbor in Valparaiso and then in her place of birth Potrero de Gallegos. On this mission, she sat and visited for hours with each. She never arrived at a house without some "obsequio" and much to talk about. These 'obsequios' were gifts; sometimes bars of Dove soap, chocolates, a blouse, a small toy for a child— humble gifts, but always given with much love. In "el Potrero" her second mission was to re-live her old life, getting up early, before the break of dawn, to help milk the cows and return to help make the tortillas and food for breakfast. Later in the day, turning her efforts to the cheese, gorditas, or cajeta-making summer tasks. She was never still and loved making the long trek to 'La Zocona' ! In that last visit she also spent precious time with life-long friends and even made it further south into Mexico to Queretaro to spend time with her brother, tio Armando and his family.

The other day my cousin recalled Ama being so 'cariñosa'. I don't know of an equivalent word in English. The only way to explain this word is with a description of my mother on this trip. 'Cariñosa', meaning she was demonstrative in her love, her tenderness, and her attentive help. To be able to give, to share, to help, to 'convivir' with all her family brought her complete joy. She demonstrated such love for all her countless relatives and friends. She especially loved and extended her cariño to her brothers, her cousins, and all their children –her nieces and nephews. Her gifts were small, but her love, her 'cariño' was boundless.

Ama was a thin petite woman and nothing about her physical body told of her strength, like her hands. Her long elegant fingers strong but rough and calloused from a lifetime of working with them. Growing up in her pueblito or what we call 'el rancho,' el Potrero de Gallegos, everything that made up daily life, everything needed to survive and thrive, was created by the work of the hands.

Because my mother was the eldest in a family of boys, she was her mother's right hand. She assisted in the care of the home and animals, the milking of the cows, the making tortillas and cheese, the planting, the sewing, and the knitting. She tended to younger brothers as babies, and learned to heal all the variety of injuries her active and mischievous brothers encountered. The hardest work all, was the washing all boys' denim clothes by hand against the rocks in the cold water of a nearby creek. All this same work continued as her brothers grew up and she raised her own children before moving to the U.S.

I remember many an evening when the dryness and rough calloused skin of her hands and feet demanded her attention and care. To soothe them, she had her own remedy, as she did for many an ailment. She would melt the wax from a candle and mix it with glycerin to rub on her hands and feet for some temporary and much needed relief.

In those evening, I missed the story her hands were telling. The truth is that in those moments, I saw her aged, tired and weathered and this frustrated me, pained me and I...simply... missed the story. The story her hands were telling was not a story of fatigue or simply a story of my mother's lifetime of work. Her hands narrated a journey of endurance and care. Her hands narrated a life of creating, nurturing, and healing her family and her beloved. Her hands made manifest a life story of what it means to love deeply in this world.

As a very young child, I had a dream that haunted me for years before my mother died. My brothers, sisters and I are standing in the kitchen surrounding my mother as she stands at the stove stirring a pot of food. The rest of the room is dark but a kitchen light glows directly over my mother's head. I'm looking up at her and am pulling at her apron trying to get her attention as she's begins serving my brothers their food. All of us are talking at once and each of us vying for her attention. In my frustration, I began pulling at her leg, until much to my horror I pull her leg off.

I try to fix it, but it's impossible. I hated this dream so much, it scared me and made me feel so guilty all at once. In my impatience and selfishness I had hurt our mother, Ama.

There is a beautiful heart wrenching song that my mother loved so much; that song was her love song for my father. It was hard for me to understand her love for him and at times of anger at how my father treated her, I'd ask her, why she didn't divorce him. She would always look at me confused at what seemed to her like such a ridiculous question and she would say, *"es mi cruz mija, es mi cruz."* He was her cross to bear, she would say. This response would anger me so much. A husband shouldn't be a cross to bear, was my thinking! That wasn't love, that wasn't love at all, it was a penance!

I realize now, I had it all wrong- what I imagined she meant and what she was really trying to say to me were two very different things. One of my uncles, Tio Armando, told me a little of my parents' courtship as youngsters; how he would whistle for her when they were both working out in the 'campo' to secretly rendezvous. He told me about the nights my mother and her brothers and my dad and his sisters sat around a campfire playing games that would offer the chance from my parents to flirt and play. He told me about how my father's long stays in the U.S. after my parents married caused my mother so much suffering. My father spent the majority of the year, every year, working in the U.S. She suffered this separation, missing my father and her love song for him was "Cruz de Olvido." The song tells of the heartache of the beloved feels at having to depart; "La barca en que me iré Lleva una cruz de olvido; Lleva una cruz de amor Y en esa cruz sin ti Me moriré de hastío." It was her favorite song. Now, I think that what she meant, her cross to bear, was the love she felt for my father. She loved this man across distance and time, through many disappointments and injury— she had loved him for a lifetime and nothing that he ever did or failed to do, could change that love.

My sister Elsa tells me that when she was growing up in El Potrero, the gardens of each house were a thing of beauty (many still are). Each homemaker took great care in saving water each day (was no running water then) to nurture and grow their splendid gardens. She said that it seemed as every home was in competition with the other and yes maybe the the ladies were a little competitive, but they were also very communal and shared plant cuttings and seeds with each other so that each home had a colorful array of flowers, useful herbs, and fruit trees to share and enjoy.

My mother brought with her not only this shared skill for gardening, but the love for nurturing beautiful gardens just as almost every person that lives here now, from El Potrero, has. As a child it amazed me (and still amazes me now) how my mother as we'd be walking back from somewhere or another, with stealth moves would cut a small portion of the plant of her desire, wrap it up and stick it in her purse. Once we got home she'd nurture the cutting over time and soon it would join the other plants and flowers in her beautiful garden.

There's a saying that if you want to be happy for a lifetime, plant a garden. Maybe this true because the work of caring for something, nurturing it, watching it grow, and observing its natural cycles, and that it gives according to the love and care that it is given is greatly satisfying and what life is all about. I think my mother not only did this with her garden, but in all her relationships with her children, her family, her comadres, her friends, and acquaintances, she nurtured them with great love and care, and this made her happy.

Ama was a healer. Not only could she alleviate a bad cold "con el bics' (Vicks vaporrub) and a tummy ache with "te de manzanilla" (chamomile tea) or "te de yerbabuena" (a mint –type tea), cramps or headaches with "te de ruda" (rue tea) like every good Mexican mother, she could also heal injuries and infections. Maybe it was a gift inherited from her grandmother or from our legendary Tia Jovita. Tia Jovita was Potrero de Gallegos' most trusted midwife and all around-medic, who had tended to almost all the births and the ailing in el rancho.

My mother started healing others early while helping care for her brothers. Tio Armando tells the story of almost hacking his toe in two with an ax that failed to hit his mark. After resisting my mom's attempt to look at it, the pain became so unbearable that he had to let her tend to it. With her careful attention she saved his toe, leaving behind only a scar. She also saved my brother Victor's finger when he sliced it picking up and throwing a piece of broken glass. As soon as we arrived home and my mother saw the bloody mess and wound across the length of his pointer finger she quickly cleaned it up. This wound probably required several stitches but much to our surprise my mom quickly located a fresh spider web, took it down and wrapped my brother's finger with it. Ask to see his finger now and you will see a very thin scar and a finger that works just fine (no stitches required). There were many other incidents that occurred in the care of her brothers and sons. There was Goyo's dislocated shoulder that she snapped back into place and his story of maggot infested wound (yes I said maggot-infested) wound, which my mother healed with her ingenuity and her skills.

If my mother went to school, it was no more than a couple of years—her learning, her education, her skills, were learned from the women that raised her, the women in her community, and the natural world around her.

Ama had a best friend. Her best friend was not only her comadre, her neighbor, a relative, but also her concuña. Her best friend, Tia Emilia was married to my father's oldest brother Tio Eloy. The two shared parallel lives, twin souls and hearts cut from the same cloth of kindness, generosity, and determination. They dealt with the same strict mother-in-law, with the same long separations from their husbands raising their children, all of similar ages, alone while their husbands were in the U.S.. But really not alone, because they had each other and truly they seemed to be one and the same.

I imagine that one of my mother's great heartbreaks when coming to the U.S. in the early 70's was leaving her best friend, Tia Emilia. Her children, my cousins, tell me they felt a great loss when our family came to the U.S. because they too were losing their best friends, all my older siblings.

Tia Emilia's love was so deep for my mother and for us that soon after my mother died and our family began to fall apart without her, Tia Emilia came from Mexico to be with us. She left her own children behind to care for us for a few months. It was like an angel had shown up at our door, an angel we knew, loved and trusted to bring us some comfort and care we desperately needed. So much like my mother, she didn't only come to care for us, she took charge of our great-grandmother and took her back to Mexico with her. My great-grandmother and her were not closely related or related at all, but she was my mother's grandmother and had been in my mother's care before she died. There was no one that could care for her like my mother, except Tia Emilia. I remember the sadness of the day Tia Emilia had to leave, return back to her own children, to my Tio Eloy back to her life in Mexico. My heart broke to see her leave, but it had to be. Our lives, our two families shaped by departures and losses but rooted, united so deeply because of their love and respect for each other.

VIVARTAKALPA

by Becca Spence Dobias

"My friend's grandpa said LA is a joke," I said, after we had figured out how to exit the airport.

"It kind of is." Noeli didn't seem disturbed. "But, I mean...it's a funny joke?"

I laughed.

"But really." Noeli grew serious. "A couple years ago I went to this Zen retreat for young adults."

"I didn't know you were into Buddhism." There were so many layers to Noeli. I would never really know all of her.

"Yeah. It sounded cool. I don't even remember how I heard about it. But I remember one of the descriptions of Buddhist cosmology. There's this Buddhist idea that there are all of these different stages or cycles of the universe, and right now we're in the lowest— as bad as it gets. The story goes that someone, a monk maybe, was asking why he had ended up here and not in a better time or place. I don't remember how he learned it, but what he figured out is that he was here in the worst of the worlds for a reason— basically to make it better." Noeli looked over at me before continuing. "I don't think this is the lowest of the low. I mean, I *know* there are harder places to be. California is a dream for my grandma. But sometimes I feel like that, about here. I feel like of all the places in the world to be, why is this the one life led me to? When I'm annoyed with the freeways and the sprawling concrete, and the filthy air, I think I'm here to learn from this, to do what I can to make community and family and do good work."

I sat with her words as I watched the cars speed past us on both sides.

"Where are we going?" I asked as we left Sunset Boulevard and got on the 101 North.

"Hiking," Noeli said.

"Hiking? You remember I'm 32 weeks pregnant and wearing Chucks, right?"

"It's a little steep but only for about a quarter mile. You can do it, I promise." Noeli exited on Laurel Canyon and followed it about a mile. She made another turn and we pulled into a large parking lot. Noeli got out three dollar bills from her thin wallet to pay the parking fee.

"It's about two and a half miles round trip," the attendant said, looking me over and pausing at my belly. "And the first part is a little steep." I took off my headband and ran my fingers through my hair.

"Yeah, we know," said Noeli.

"Have you been here before?" I asked as we walked toward the trail.

"Nope," Noeli said.

One hundred yards in and we were both panting. Noeli pulled a bottle of water from her messenger bag and handed it to me.

"Thanks," I huffed. "How far is a quarter mile?"

"I have no idea," Noeli said. "But I don't think it's too far. Look—" she pointed. "The path kind of levels off up there."

A woman, probably in her 60's, passed us, walking her dog, a little terrier in a yellow shirt.

"Ok." I willed myself to keep walking up the wide dusty path. It took us 20 minutes, I was waddling so slowly, stopping every few feet to take a big swig from the water bottle.

We reached the top of the incline and I rested my hands on my knees and took some deep breaths.

"Are you ok?" Noeli put a hand on my back, breathing heavily too. "I guess I underestimated that. And how out of shape I am."

We both laughed and I stood up, resting my hands on my lower back. I looked out over a broad expanse of green desert-y shrubs and trees. It did not look like the LA I knew. Further down, beyond the trees and shrubs, was a wide panorama. "That's the San Fernando Valley," Noeli said, gazing out too.

"It's beautiful."

"I know." Noeli paused. "If we keep walking, I guess there's a hidden rainforest trail...or...we could just sit here for a while."

We looked at each other and cracked up.

I eased myself to sitting on the side of the trail, looking out over the valley and Noeli sat next to me and took a deep breath.

"This used to be Mexico," she said eventually. "In the 1800s, there was the Mexican American War and California became part of the US. It's kind of really similar to what happened with the Native Americans in Appalachia."

"You were reading about Appalachian history?" I asked.

"I was reading the Wikipedia page." Noeli laughed and continued. "So then during the gold rush, LA supplied a bunch of the food for the miners. There was actually all kinds of farming here until everything changed to housing tracts in the 1940s. Then there were railroads and oil. There was this whole battle over the LA River and how to manage it. The Port of Long Beach is one of the biggest ways stuff gets to the United States from overseas. And you know Olvera Street? With the cactus candy?"

I nodded.

"It was this whole political thing making it in the 20s. It helped this guy from the LA Times control what the angry Mexicans were saying because it kept it in one spot and it made this place where people could see these 'well-behaved' Mexicans instead of workers who were pissed about how they were treated."

I listened, interested, but waiting for her to get to why she had brought me there. She paused and looked out over the valley again.

"I just want you to know it's a real place. It's not…pretend."

"I know," I said.

"It's not a joke," Noeli said.

"I know."

She bit her lower lip and ran her fingers through her curls.

"I think I'll always be a person from there looking at here," I said, finally.

"You can be both," Noeli said. "You can be from there and from here."

"I kind of feel like I'm in like...this hero's journey but without the return. Isn't that the climax of the whole thing?" I leaned back on one hand and felt my belly with the other. The baby was moving.

"Actually, I think the climax is the 'resurrection' in the hero's journey—the last big test before the return," Noeli said.

"Ok, Ms. English major." I rolled my eyes and nudged her shoulder with my own.

Noeli grinned and we continued to look out over the valley.

"I think there are other ways to return," Noeli said finally. "You don't have to actually go back."

"Like how?" I asked.

"In the hero's journey it's the 'return with the elixer,' right? You bring what you found back to everyone at home. So for my mom, she sends money back to my aunts and uncles in Mexico. And with your dissertation, you wrote about people from your home and you sent that knowledge back to them."

"Hm," I said, thinking.

"But also," Noeli continued. "You tell your kids about home. Do you know how many times I've heard the song 'Besame Mucho'?" And every Mexican folk and mariachi song? I know the life story of every single relative we have in Mexico even though I see them maybe once every five years. You just make your home a part of your kids too."

I nodded, pursing my lips.

We sat for a long time, staring out over the trees, until the light started to dim and the valley lit up with millions of lights, shining like so many stars.

HAND IN MARRIAGE-THE LETTER

by Cindi Neisinger

Dear Grandfather Longino,

I found this 68 year old letter you wrote, in my 85 year old mother's decades old file cabinet, in a 1969 income tax envelope. So random and ironic! Your daughter (my Mother) Dorita is still unorganized. LoL! That means (laugh-out-loud) lots has changed since you were here, Grandfather. We mostly use texting, emoji's, GIF's and emails now. I won't even bore you with social media. So you see, this letter shows me a time when people actually had individuality with fancy learned penmanship, for conversations through corespondents, as one of a few ways to the communicate. It could only be fate that I would find this letter that changed our family's world! I relish the clues you left me of a bygone era. Umm! I can be a tad-bit dramatic grandfather.

Mom remembers that this letter was overdue. Why did you wait so long to respond? Time to question my mother. 🤔(that's an emoji).

You wrote this in April of 1951, but she was ready to get married the year before. All the plans were in place for a wedding in August 1950. All you had to do is respond to my dad's, fathers, request for permission of my mom's hand in marriage to my dad. Why did you drag your feet? Is it because she was your baby girl? Mom says she was your "nina." I know you and grandmother owned a general store in Los Angeles during the depression, after you came from Mexico, where you helped many with credit during a dark time in our history. Mom recalls when she was a young girl, you would nap, and she would prank you. One day, she applied lipstick and kissed your face all over, than she put earrings, a bandana, and finished, with a crazy hair do. She woke you up with a mirror and you exclaimed, "Ay mija que me asiste?" (Oh daughter what did you do to me?) While howling with laughter. Yes! she was your little girl. I get it. But, I'm glad you wrote this letter. I was born because you decided begrudgingly, to respond, yes. So are many generations that followed. Grateful!

Benito and Dorita were happily married August 5th, 1951.

Oh! Grandfather Longino, you passed before I was born but this treasure endears me as a reminder of a chivalrous era when there were eloquent manners. I admire how you wrote in a formal style with a rich vocabulary and beautiful penmanship. What an honor to have met you through this letter and the memories of my mother.

Well, Grandfather maybe someone will find my letter to you on the internet. Probably, misfiled somewhere in cyberspace.

I love you,

Cindi

Your granddaughter (from Dorita, your Nina)

P.S. You are a Great, Great, Great, Grandfather in 2017! ♡

My two Grandfathers were born in Mexico. One migrating to Los Angeles, California, in the 1920's. The other came to the USA in 1954. The letter is written by my Mother's Father, Longino Gutierrez to my Dad's Father, Fabian Caldera, confirming his approval of their marriage. My Mom said she had all the plans in place a year before but her father would not respond. Till she over heard my grandmother, telling him, "It is time Longino!"

I only met my Grandfather Fabian as a child (My dads' father) and I loved him very much. What a wonderful loving Grandfather he was...so much kindness, hugs, ice cream and the best Menudo ever! And he always wore a hat.

INVISIBLE IMMIGRANT

by Judy Kohnen

When I took out American Citizenship, four years ago, it had an unintended consequence. I suddenly felt like I had a home. It was a ridiculous feeling because I had lived in Claremont, California for over twenty years as an immigrant and never once felt like I belonged in the States, yet as soon as that American passport arrived in the mail, I felt security. It helped me figure out how to belong. Today, I am more comfortable living undercover as an invisible immigrant. Invisible because everyone assumes I was born American because I am white and I speak fluent English with a mid-west accent.

The first time I felt the weight of an identity crisis was when I was thirteen years old, standing on a street corner, waiting to cross chaotic Tehran traffic. There was disquiet everywhere. My headscarf was slipping and I adjusted it to tuck in my blonde, Farah Fawcett curls. The hairstyle was all the rage but it was first time in five years in Iran that I covered my hair. A tank faced me, adjacent from my position at the roundabout, its long gun angled crookedly down the main street. It seemed to be unmanned, but tanks were normally dormant during the day, it was at night when the tanks rumbled out their grinding earthquake tremors while patrolling the streets to maintain the Shah's curfew.

As I waited for the traffic cop to signal me across the street, I watched a shopkeeper clean out his store. He took down a picture of the Shah Pahlavi and his family, leaving an empty square of clean paint etched on the wall. Before placing the frame with paperwork and books inside a cardboard box, he carefully rubbed dust off the glass. The shopkeeper was mournful looking, and when his rheumy eyes caught mine, he held up a gnarled finger to his lips, and then pointed to the monument in the middle of the roundabout. Assembled around the foot of the statue of Reza Shah was a collection of cardboard boxes. The statue had his hand raised in a salute, or benevolent wave, and a thin rope was draped around one shoulder and looped across one arm.

The shopkeeper was not cleaning his shop. The boxes were being collected as fuel for a bonfire. They were going to pull down the statue and burn everything. In that moment, I felt the smallness of being a child, invisible and insignificant within the machination of events larger than myself. I ran home, my heart thumping, knowing that my parents should not leave me alone on the streets but grateful that Mum let me visit my two friends. Their mother, Mrs. Prentiss, was the drama teacher at my British-Iranian school, Rustam Abadian, I loved their animated household full of irreverent laughter. When we came back from Christmas break, I wanted to continue to ingratiate myself with the older sisters so I could sit with them on the school bus.

But I never saw them again.

The experience at the roundabout was scary, in an exciting way, but I never told my mother what I saw. I did not want to break the pantomime of business as usual. Parents and teachers assured children that there was nothing to fear, as if children did not notice unusual happenings; the chanting on rooftops, the BBC reports of riots, fathers not going to work, tank patrols, electricity shortages and bathtubs full of water. We were told that school was closing early for the holidays and people were leaving on vacation until things calmed down. Who were we to tell them otherwise, or not trust in their counsel?

Not long after, my family left Iran in December 1978, arriving before Christmas at a tiny flat that belonged to my mother's auntie in England. We had twenty-two suitcases, crammed with Persian carpets and copper pots. In those days, there were hundreds of displaced engineers looking for work in the oil and natural gas industry and anticipation of the unknown continued while we waited for Dad to find a job and my sisters and I were enrolled in school in Woking, Surrey.

In Iran, I was one of many expatriates with a funny accent and a cultural background that differentiated us from one another. I was the Canadian. There was a family of white Africans from Rhodesia. There was a black African, I think he had also left Rhodesia. My Indian girlfriend had the best British accent. This Iranian was Jewish. That Iranian was the youngest son of the shah. This Iranian was Armenian. That Iranian received house calls at night from the SAVAK, the secret police. This other Iranian friend was related to the rulers of Pakistan who had been executed. In those well-travelled circles, everyone was different, everyone had a story and we were all the same because of those stories.

But in England, I felt very exposed as a foreigner. Whenever I asked a question, the locals jovially referred to me as a colonial. At school, the kids whistled *Yankee Doodle Dandy* when I rounded the corridors. I did not know what a Yankee was, but I knew it was nothing honorable. In Iran, during the months of unrest, my mother found a business card pressed into her hand when she was shopping at the bazaar. In uneven type, with a spelling mistake, it read, *Yonkee, go home.* My mother was appalled, and not by the typo.

"I am not a Yankee," she yelled after the disappearing figure who had slipped her the card, "I am British!"

That's how I knew a Yankee was nothing to be admired and of course, being teased about it did not help. My best guess was that Yankees were Italian-Americans because they liked to eat macaroni but I was confused. I carried a Canadian passport, and Yankees were North American too, I could only hope that Canadians and Yankees were not related. Teasing at school did not last long because as soon as I started to make friends, we moved. We had been in England for four months, but it felt much longer.

Our next stop was France. In France, I let people classify me as an American because I finished the school year at the American School of Paris. I was an Anglophone, born in Alberta and none of my relatives spoke French, or even liked the French. Besides, it was way too tedious to face the apoplectic incredulity when I explained to Frenchmen that I was a Canadian who did not speak French. They all expected a Quebecer. The following September, my parents enrolled me in a French school. Four years later, I graduated the Lycee as a Canadian who spoke French with a Parisian accent.

By this time, I was curious about Canada. I wrote a heartfelt college essay about wanting to find my roots and was accepted at McGill University in Montreal. Once there, I was recognized as a Francophone from France, an accolade I enjoyed, but after three winters, I was depressed and not really fitting in. My taproot was frozen. The good news was my Canadian boyfriend, a guy who was born in Germany, raised in French-Canada, and who wore a cross-cultural hat like I did. He had found an internship at Harvey Mudd College in Southern California. It was warm there and the mountains reminded me of Iran. The guy was cute too. After a summer visit I moved in with him. My parents had relocated to Indonesia and were too far away to object. Besides, I would not stay for long,

But I was wrong.

I married the cute guy, had children and was stuck in Claremont, a Very

Nice Place to Raise Kids. It was a beautiful, boring community. Getting my green card was a slow and irritating process and the whole time I waited for the next opportunity to move. All those international transitions made me a Third Culture Kid. I identified less with my birth country, a bit with my mother's British culture and a whole lot with the Iranian culture because I spent a significant amount of my early childhood development in Iran and it had been a positive experience. I knew more about Iranian food, history and manners than I knew about American or Canadian politics, TV or culture. I could carry my home on my back, like a turtle, but I did not have a home or belong in Iran, England, France, Canada or the United States. It was painful to make friendships with others who did not share similar mobile experiences. My isolation was compounded by the fact that I looked and sounded American. On the surface, Americans seemed warm and effusive with their perfect teeth and beaming smiles and phrases like "nice to meet you" or "let's have coffee" but it was a polite remark, they never followed through, unless it was for business. Americans were wholly consumed by their activities. Americans were busy people, very earnest and family oriented, but they had no time for others.

British or Canadian culture is a "near culture" to America, but there are differences. Differences that affected my behavior. I learned to spell in American English. I kept my dry British wit and sarcastic humor under wraps because it tended to offend Americans. I engaged Americans too quickly by asking for their opinions or political views, so I stopped talking and tried to smile more with my yellow, British teeth. Whenever I walked into a room I scanned for interesting people, first for Persians, then for British, then for any travelers or foreigners, then for Americans with a multi-cultural background. Last of all would be white American who could pull together a personal and telling story. Something informative, naughty or intellectual. I craved differences. I was very scornful of people who wanted rules or homogeneity. Americans seemed very plain. Bland was boring.

Growing up between countries leaves an imprint on the psyche, and my response to those many losses and change was a shield to protect myself. Military, diplomatic, missionary kids have this struggle, and any children who have moved every three years or so. Making and losing friends, leaving schools, teachers and pets behind created hidden trauma and instability. In truth, it wasn't ever about the Americans. It was all about me. I did not want to invest in friendships or generate roots because my experience taught me it would not be for long. I'd be moving away. Saying goodbye hurts, whereas changing gears for a new place is excitement. I assumed all

Americans had deep and meaningful friendships but were purposefully not sharing it. I wanted a culturally satisfying relationship so much that I became needy and unrealistic. I wanted to fix everything so I could to live in harmony, and yet I hated my boring life. I put a good foot forward, was very capable, but I got depressed often. I created my own unhappiness.

When I got my American passport, I was ready to stop pretending that I would soon leave America to go somewhere better. Since I was not a global nomad, I had to develop the sense of belonging that I craved. I would act as if I were going to die in Claremont and leave my little house feet first. If that were true, what would I change? I started by making my home my own. I landscaped my front yard to showcase my love of succulents. A few years later, I tore out my living room and redecorated it in a way that would make me happier to live there forever. This was no longer a starter home or a transitional stop. I tended to the things that made me feel secure. I allowed myself to become more committed to my community. I valued local friendships and I stopped making fast and snobby judgments about others. I stopped hanging on to unreasonable results (launching teenagers helped with that last one.)

Once I was more relaxed, I discovered that everyone incubates their own culture. Everyone carries around their own inner culture through their heritage, their race, or a religious group. This shows up in the food they eat, their manners, jokes, clothes etc. When one American marries another American they squabble over food preparation, over traditions and ways to do things, because they come from different family cultures, too. They end up blending the best of each culture, just like my husband and I did. Americans were interesting people after all. Culture was still a perennial fascination for me, as are the associated concepts of identity, belonging, grief, and loss, but it no longer narrowed my vision; instead it magnified the richness of life around me.

Today, I get my multi-cultural kicks by helping Syrian refugees settle into America. I know what it is like to lose your home and friendships due to political events outside your control. I understand the value of a kind welcome. The refugees arrive with only one or two suitcases, like I did, but unlike me, they have a legal work visa and quite a bit more faith in America.

Becoming an American is journey. Eventually, you meet yourself on the path of your life. You will see what happened in the past, you will see dark shadows underneath, and you will notice things about you that are invisible to others but are the cultural values that guide like a shining beacon, as well as the perceptions and beliefs that hold you back. You will recognize that for every strength there is an opposing weakness, that you need support to be independent, and that there are more perceptions than truths. I have yet to meet the perfect American, only people with positions and values, informed by culture and their reactions to events.

So what? I have the thoughts of a Brit, the spirit of a Western Canadian and a huge delight in all things Persian but if you never know these things about me, you will know that I am American. I may be an invisible immigrant, but I have developed a strong American identity. I no longer feel invisible.

A Syrian refugee taught me my progress the other day. Every Syrian woman practices the ancient Middle Eastern art of hospitality. They serve strong Turkish coffee in wee cups, fruit and baklava before any serious conversation. (Persians do the same but they prefer tea served in tiny glasses.) The first Arabic words I ever learned were schway-schway "slow, slow." Syrians always tell me to slow down. I was getting restless and checking the time when my host looked up at me. She'd been in the United States for over eight months and her English was better than most.

"You busy." she nodded to me, knowingly. Then she smiled. "Next year, I hope I be all the time busy. Then I be American woman, just like you!"

KISSING COUSINS

by Ellen Estilai

March 2006

It was 2 a.m. in Tehran, but behind Mehrabad Airport's glass doors, we saw hundreds of people waiting in the darkness beyond the barricades, anxiously scanning the long line of arriving passengers for their friends and relatives. Suddenly people surged forward from the crowd in front of us, laughing, shrieking, holding out their arms, embracing the four of us, kissing us on both cheeks. Maybe fifteen people...no...twenty-five—they just kept coming toward us, all wide grins and shining eyes—all those Estilai faces. This giddy throng engulfed us one by one. I stopped myself just in time before I kissed a complete stranger by mistake—a man, an innocent bystander waiting for another family. In the Islamic Republic of Iran, where unrelated members of the opposite sex may not even shake hands in public, this would have been an inauspicious beginning.

My husband Ali's nephews looked at our four baggage carts and sprang into action, dividing them up among the available vehicles. Hossein, a seasoned veteran of airport arrivals, had hired a small pick-up truck to carry the bulk of our luggage. Everyone piled into five cars and took off for the apartment that my brother-in-law Ghasem had made ready for us, where we sat until five a.m., drinking tea and telling each other how we couldn't believe we were here. "This is like a dream," they said. "We had almost given up hope."

Almost twenty-six years had passed since Ali and I and our daughters Samira and Sarah were in Mehrabad Airport together— July 29, 1980, Samira's birthday. After eight years under the Shah and a tumultuous year of the Islamic Republic of Iran, we had decided to return to the United States, at least temporarily. But when we were about to board the plane, the authorities would not let Ali leave. They gave no reason.

"You have to take the children," he said, as he thrust our travel documents in my hand. "I'll join you when I can."

It was seventy days of fear and uncertainty before we would be reunited in California. For far too many years after that, Samira's birthday would include a rehash of the worst day of our lives. For a long time, the story remained painful and immediate. It became our family legend, recited annually until these recitations faded into a kind of shorthand and finally into no words at all. Gradually, it dawned on us that it was unfair to Samira to have these memories play any role in her celebration, so we put those thoughts aside and let her have her day, unencumbered by the weight of that sadness and disappointment and fear. But we did not forget any of it

But now, for Ali and me, the worst was over. Any fears of customs agents, airport police and Revolutionary Guards proved to be unfounded. However, for Samira and Sarah, the real stress had just begun. Although well out of graduate school, they were now suddenly overtaken with middle school angst. Like seventh graders on the first day of school, they wondered if they would fit in with The Beautiful Cousins.

The twenty or so relatives crowded into this small apartment were just the advance party. Another two hundred or so were waiting in Ali's home city, Kerman. On their Iranian side, our daughters had six aunts and uncles and twenty-nine first cousins. These first cousins had forty-one children, many of them close in age to our daughters. Twenty-four of those first cousins and thirty-eight of their children were in Iran. Since we left in 1980, the girls had seen most of them only in grainy, jerky, unmodulated videos of family celebrations—weddings, birthdays, Iranian New Year parties.

For the last twenty-five years, the four of us have celebrated Nowruz, the Iranian New Year, in California, sprouting wheat, dying eggs, taking photos around the traditional *haft sin* table laid with dried jujubes, garlic, vinegar, sprouted wheat spread, apples and other things that begin with the Persian letter *sin,* which corresponds to the letter S in English. We would gather together each March 20, at whatever time the vernal equinox occurred that year—at ten in the morning, or five in the afternoon or midnight. We would turn on the Iranian television station and wait for the countdown. We would help jam the phone lines to Iran, calling our relatives in Kerman and Tehran with Nowruz wishes, saying *yes, ensha'allah, perhaps next year we will be there...yes, we will try...yes, we miss you, too.*

And we did miss them. Our own Nowruz celebrations were bittersweet. Sure, we stocked up on Iranian pastries from the bakeries in Tehrangeles or Orange County. I made *sabzi polow ba mahi*, the traditional herbed pilaf with fish. But there was no massive *khooneh takooni*—literally, shaking of the house—that month-long spring cleaning marathon during which the entire country turns itself inside out and back again, banishing winter's sooty, grimy bleakness. No *chahar shanbe soori*, jumping over burning sagebrush on the last Tuesday night of the year, exchanging one's winter sallowness for the fire's red glow. No two-week holiday with *deed o baz deed*, visiting and being visited in return. No round of lunches and dinners, no picnics in the country beside a running stream on *sizdah be dar*, the thirteenth day of the New Year, when it's bad luck to stay indoors.

In 1987, a relative brought back a Nowruz video from Iran that wasn't compatible with our system. We searched the Los Angeles Iranian Yellow Pages for a company that could convert the video to a U.S. format and found a small shop on Westwood Boulevard, tucked away amid the Iranian restaurants and travel agencies, waxing salons, bakeries and bookstores. As soon as we mounted the narrow stairs to the second-floor shop, I was transported back to Tehran. The owner, an Iranian immigrant who had been a film director during the shah's era, had succeeded in recreating, like a movie set, a particularly Iranian business environment: the drab office, complete with dingy gray walls, unmatched metal furniture, Iranian movie posters from the 70s, and the unmistakable aura of abandoned dreams.

He promised to have our video ready by the following week. However, we got busy and put off making the ninety-minute drive to pick it up. After a few weeks, the shop owner left a message in Persian on our answering machine: "Ali Agha," he said, as one might say to an old friend, "aren't you coming to pick up your video? These people are singing songs to you and crying for you." Not only had he converted the video, he had sat and watched all ninety minutes of it, and he couldn't understand how we could be so cavalier.

When we got the tape home, we understood his sense of urgency. Fifty or so relatives had gathered in my brother-in-law Reza's house to send us messages—songs that Ali himself used to sing, or songs that they had modified to fit the situation. His sister Naazi sang, "Patience and happiness left with my brother," instead of "with my beloved." His brother Reza sang lines of melancholy poetry Ali had written decades before—and hadn't thought of for years. Small children recited nursery rhymes. The elders introduced the newest members of the family, the babies, the new fiancée. Reza's wife Pouran said, "We hope you will call so we can hear your voices. We hope you will teach Samira and Sarah Persian so we can talk to them. We hope we'll be together again."

Over the years, all the videos the family sent us had a certain sameness. Watching them was like attending one long progressive dinner party during which fashions changed and faces aged. The perimeter of the room was usually the province of the older folks, who arranged themselves along the walls, grudgingly acknowledging the camera; the center of the room was throbbing with younger family members vying for the camera's attention. Samira and Sarah would follow these installments with great interest, as if they were watching the stars of a reality show, *The Real Cousins of Kerman*. As they watched their generation grow up in these videos, they would pay particular attention to the clothes and hairstyles, the singing and dance moves, the good-natured teasing, the emergence of beards and mustaches, the flicking of long tresses. But most of all, they studied the closeness the cousins seemed to share. For Iranians, even a second cousin once removed can be as close as a brother or sister. Sarah felt that watching these videos was like watching a party they hadn't been invited to. But of course, they had always been invited. They just hadn't shown up for twenty-six years.

When we first decided to make the trip, Samira was filled with a sense of dread, which she tactfully kept to herself. She was afraid that Ali and I might be arrested and taken away. Those feelings she had as a young child when her father couldn't leave Iran with us came back to her with such force that she shut down and avoided talking about our plans. However, once our new Iranian passports arrived and she saw her face, encircled by hijab, staring out at her from the official document, she became more engaged. Still, it wasn't until American friends started asking her why she was going to Iran, of all places, that she was finally able to articulate her thoughts and admit to herself that she really wanted to go—and why. She wanted to see her family, she told her friends. She wanted to see her cousins and the children of her cousins.

Both girls had always felt a pull, a longing for family when they watched the Iranian videos, a sense that they had missed out by not having these "automatic friendships." They knew the names and faces of the players in this long-running show, but few details of the plot.

They would need subtitles for that.

Before we left Iran in 1980, seven-year-old Samira and five-year old Sarah spoke Persian fluently. Whenever we returned from a visit to the States, the children always had a period of transition from English back to Persian, but after two weeks, they were chattering away as if they had never left Iran. Persian was their mother tongue, even if it wasn't their mother's. Those nine years we lived in Iran, we spoke primarily Persian at home because it was just easier. The relatives who visited frequently did not speak English, and we didn't want to leave anyone out of the conversation. The girls went to Persian-language schools. Ali and I read to them in Persian.

But when we moved back to the States, that dynamic was reversed. By the time Ali was able to leave Iran and join us in Claremont, the children were already in school and totally immersed in English. When Ali tried to speak with them in Persian, they resisted. "Whaaaat?" they would say in response to every Persian overture. This disheartening response annoyed him no end. He tried for a few weeks and then gave up.

After we moved to Riverside five years later, an Iranian friend offered to hold weekly Persian language classes. The girls studied for a few months but quickly tired of it. Ali and I didn't insist, but over the years, we chastised ourselves for giving in so easily. Years later, Samira took some Persian language classes at university, but neither she nor Sarah was comfortable speaking Persian. Their mother tongue had withered. They had a few isolated words but no way to string them together. Now that they were in their thirties, we all saw the error of our ways. They were worried that their cousins would make fun of them; they were worried they wouldn't be able to connect.

For Samira and Sarah, the first few days in Iran were filled with awkward smiles and silences. The turning point came at the Nowruz celebration in Kerman at Reza and Pouran's house. When the dancing started, Samira and Sarah found themselves stuck in a middle school nightmare, huddled on one side of the room with all of the cool kids on the other. The cool kids had sheer numbers on their side but were just as unsure about how to approach these American cousins. Finally the two most outgoing of the bunch, Salimeh and Mehdi, pulled Samira and Sarah into the undulating throng. The middle school spell was broken. Over the next four weeks, under the cousins' tutelage, Samira and Sarah's language skills improved along with their dance moves.

They were fortunate to have this handy form of non-verbal communication at almost every dinner party. Before the revolution, I don't remember anyone dancing at Estilai family gatherings. However, twenty-six years later, everyone was moving to the beat, even the elders. The Islamic government had banned dancing in public, but that didn't stop people from rolling up the rugs and cutting loose at home. In fact, it probably encouraged it.

Now that the ice was broken, Samira and Sarah had to endure the good-natured ribbing that comes with being an Estilai. Their cousins teased them about how tightly they had tied their headscarves when we first arrived and how little make-up they wore.

They gave them a crash course in Iranian youth culture. They took them to teahouses and showed them how to smoke water pipes. They showed them how to artfully drape their headscarves and introduced them to their favorite Iranian techno pop and rap artists. Anxious to practice their English, they traded Persian idioms for American ones.

Ali was delighted to see how easily Samira and Sarah fit in with their cousins and the rest of the family. It soon became clear that, language attrition aside, our daughters had retained much of their Iranian-ness—their basic courtesy, respect for elders, interest in Iranian culture, and most of all, love of family.

We enjoyed watching the family's surprised reactions to them. Shamsi, their Uncle Ahmad's wife, made no secret of her sense of relief. For the last 26 years, she had worried that Samira and Sarah would be lost to them. "I was afraid they would forget about us," she confided.

But I think it wasn't just the effects of all those miles and years that she feared; it was also her idea of the cultural divide. Many Iranians assume that Americans have little use for family. They think we all throw our oafish, churlish children out of the house when they reach 18 and warehouse our aging parents in drab assisted living facilities. Some of our parents are warehoused and some of our children are indeed oafish, but most of us have the same standards and make the same sacrifices for family that Iranians do. I don't know if that image of the cold, callous American family is more the fault of American media or the Iranian government's anti-American rants, but it is a prevalent stereotype.

Several years ago, we met up in Palm Springs with Shamsi's sister Najmeh, who was visiting from her home in Vancouver, BC. We were lounging on piles of rugs, sipping tea in a Persian carpet store when Samira began to complain of a sore throat. "Don't worry," I said. "Have some more tea, and I'll make you soup when we get home."

"Wow! Just like an Iranian mother," said Najmeh. She was laughing when she said this, but she was clearly surprised, as if an American mother wouldn't subscribe to the healing powers of soup or cater to a sick child in her thirties.

Ali's nephew Mohammad Reza once told me that my sense of obligation to family is the result of living among Iranians. At first, I bristled at that suggestion. I would like to think that I would have been this way whether or not I had married into an Iranian family and lived in Iran, but there might be some truth in what he says. Living among the Estilais has changed me, expanding whatever meager capacity I had for sacrifice and forgiveness, for give and take, for entertaining drop-in guests for a month or two, and making intimate dinners for fifteen.

It's impossible to know exactly how much of me is American and how much is Iranian, but one thing is certain: I can't resist the lure of my Iranian family. It was the same for Samira and Sarah. For them, the success of that trip to Iran was all about connecting with their Iranian family, birthplace, first language, and former selves, and maybe even the selves they might have been had they stayed.

One afternoon during our visit to Kerman, Samira and Sarah ventured into the bazaar with their cousin Mehdi and ran into their Aunt Naazi outside an ice cream parlor. They all felt how special this meeting was. On the surface, it was an ordinary encounter complete with squeals of recognition, kisses, pleasantries, and cups of *faludeh* (starchy vermicelli topped with rosewater or lemon juice), but its very ordinariness was extraordinary because it happened after 26 years of separation. *This is what it would be like if we lived here. This is what it is like to be a Real Cousin of Kerman.*

Excerpted from *Exit Prohibited*, a memoir-in-progress

I WANT TO BE AN AMERICAN

by Ivan Riascos

Artist Statement:

"I Want to be an American" relates to identity and the need for assimilation to its surrounding dominant culture, because of insecurities that stem from being a child of Colombian immigrants. Through the use of photographs I show a physical alteration in 4 stages, similar to documenting the after results of plastic surgery. The genre of photography I use to show this process are the typical class photos taken at the beginning of the school year. I specifically used my class photos of Grades 1, 3, 4, and 5.

The physical transformations also reflect the period moving from the city of San Fernando, California (Mexican populated area) to Forest City, Florida (White populated area). I attended Morning Side Elementary located in San Fernando, California until the 3rd grade. Grades 4-5 were taken in Forest City Elementary, Longwood, FL.

The titles of the art correspond with the slow transformation. I wanted to legally change my name to Scott Smith, so I would be accepted by the surrounding society.

Ivan Riascos, I Want to be an American (Photo series)

1st Grade (Ivan Manuel Riascos) Page 137

3rd Grade (Ivan Riascos) Page 138

4th Grade (John Riascos) Page 139

5th Grade (John Scott) Page 140

The move was very difficult for me since I was in the minority; only a few Latin children attended my school. White children were the predominant race. The Latin community was very small at the time in Central Florida unlike San Fernando. I so desperately wanted to fit into the surrounding white culture that I witnessed not only in my surrounding community but also from what I saw TV and heard on the radio.

Eventually I got to know my culture and love myself that I understood what being an American really meant.

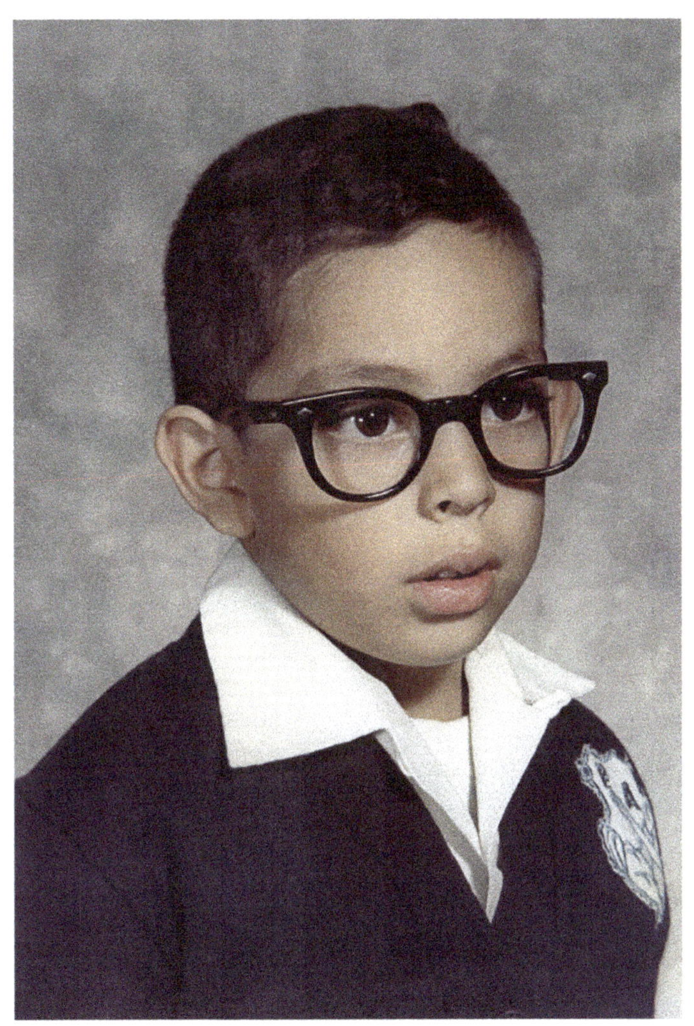

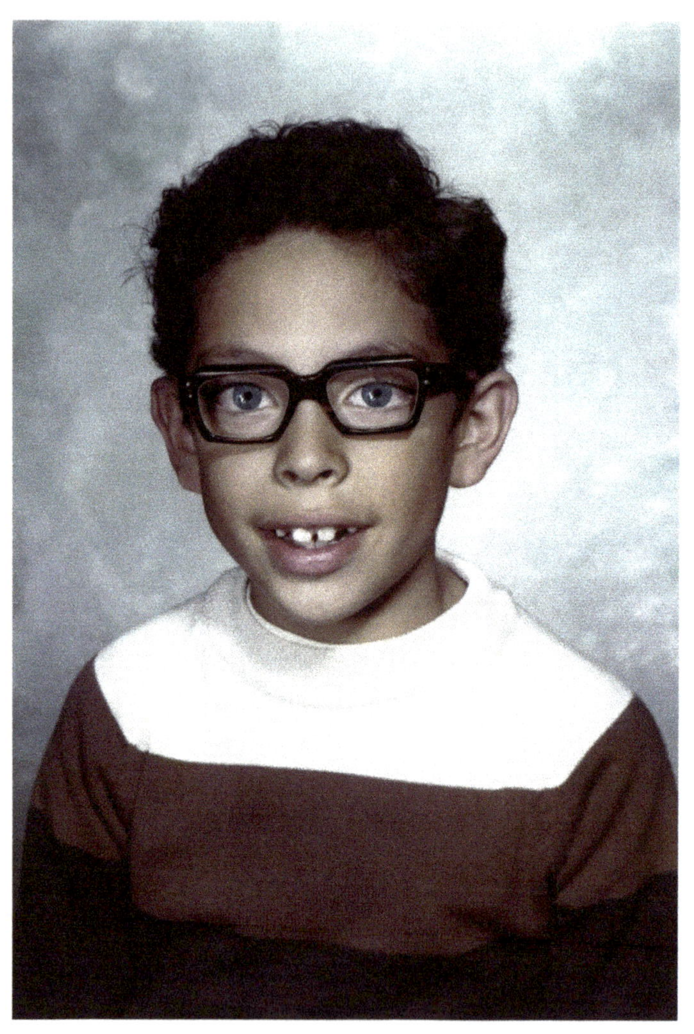

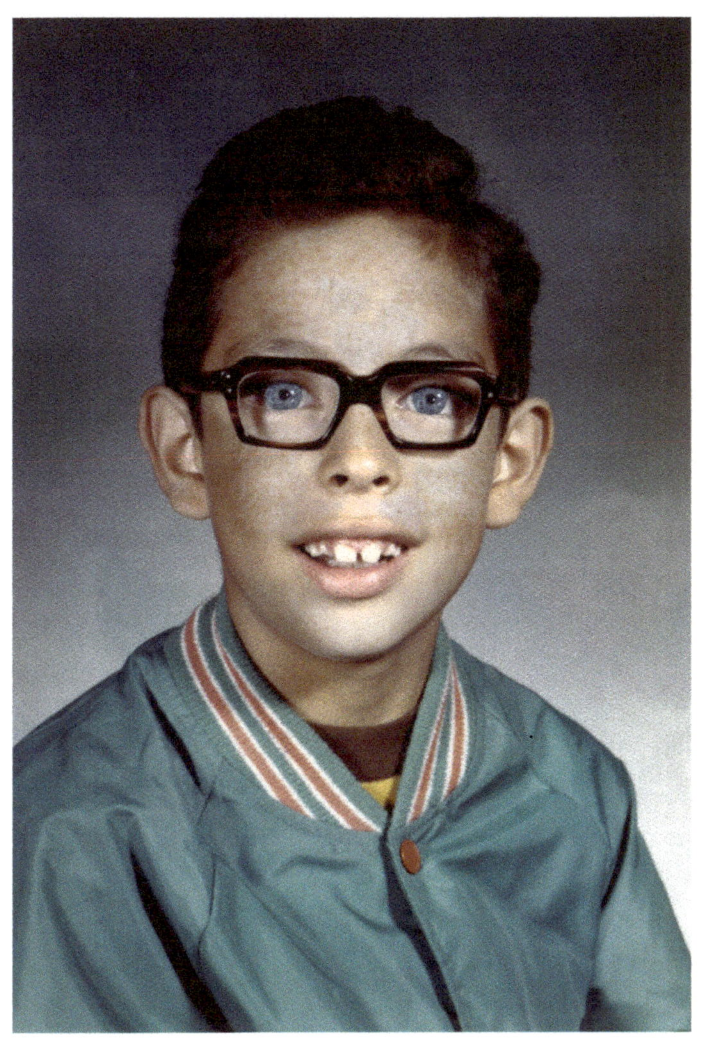

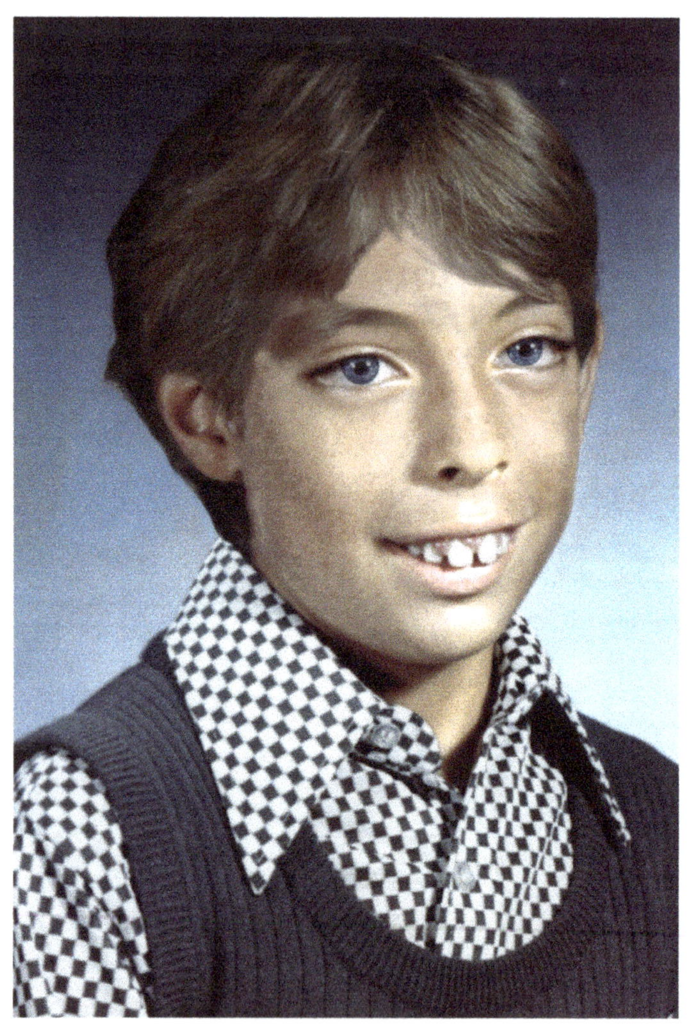

PILGRIMAGE TO SONORA

by Frances J. Vasquez

Sonora querida, tierra consentida de dicha y placer
extraño tu suelo y sufro mi anhelo por volverte a ver....
— Adolfo Huerta

The nostalgic lyrics of "Sonora Querida"—an old Mexican song I learned when I was a child—played like a soundtrack in my anxious mind. My evocative theme song played as I rode on *el Corre Caminos* bus en route to Tijuana. Like a mantra, the song helped placate my fears on a visceral level during my angst-filled winter sojourn to be with my ailing mother Rosa Lidia Valenzuela—in her beloved homeland: Ciudad Obregón, Sonora, México.

The transport, popular with nacionales, took me to Tijuana International Airport for an emergency trip to Ciudad Obregón. It was urgent that I travel to Sonora to see my gravely ill mother. I prayed to God and the Blessed Mother for her recovery, "*Diosito Querido! Madre Mía; please heal my Mamá.*" I pleaded with a heavy heart—fearing the worst.

Making travel arrangements was a challenge, as I could not find a timely domestic flight to Ciudad Obregón from Los Angeles or Ontario. Obregón is not a popular, touristy destination—thus limiting travel options. None of the flights originating Stateside offered direct flights. All had multiple connections —some flights took as long as 18-24 hours. Travel by train or bus were not feasible either, as these modes would take too long. The itinerary I selected would be the fastest, most efficient way to get to my Mamá's homeland. Not knowing when I would return, I booked a direct one-way flight with Volaris Airlines out of Tijuana.

My theme song dominated my thoughts, "*Sonora querida, tierra consentida de dicha y placer, extraño tu suelo y sufro mi anhelo por volverte a ver...*" The poetic lyrics exalt the cultural and geographic treasures of the state of Sonora. It extols the beauty of its women; it praises the fiery Bacanora (Agave-based liquor) that ignites the passions. The song lauds significant places, including Obregón: a southwest Sonoran city in *el Valle del Yaqui* where my mother resides—clinging vicariously to life.

In silent contemplation, I alternated between prayers and my theme song. As if performing in a surreal movie, I reviewed my loving, yet complex relationship with Mamá over the years. My fretful thoughts were punctuated with twinges of remorse for what was... and for what could have been. I was already grieving. I lamented not making more contact as of late with my mother. I felt sad for not being able to visit her for the New Year, when Mamá was still lucid and in relatively good health. I reflected somberly, "*Diosito, why did I sustain the eye injury which derailed my travel expectations during the Christmas Holiday season*?"

I worried that this journey to México could be the last time I would see Mamá. I reflected on the desperate Face Book messages that my niece Milagros posted regarding Mamá's acute illness and hospitalization.

My sister Dora informed me tearfully by telephone that Mamá's prognosis was grave. She implored, "*Ven pronto a Obregón...* ". Mamá was not expected to survive the acute pneumonia and bronchitis that ravaged her 88-year old body. Hospital doctors advised our Sonoran family that Rosa Lidia only had a few hours to live, or at best, a few days. Her heart was weak. One kidney no longer functioned. She was unable to breathe on her own. Doctors told our family to begin preparations for Mamá's funeral. Dora asked me to speak to Mamá, hoping that by hearing my voice, it might uplift her. Dora placed the phone to Mamá's ear and I told her to fight for her life—that it was not her time to go; that God still had plans for her. I conveyed to Mamá that I was leaving immediately to see her. "*Lucha y dále ganas a la vida, Mamá, porque te queremos mucho, y te necesitamos. Te quiero, Mamá*". Afterwards, Dora told me that our mother visibly responded with a faint smile.

My sister Leonore couldn't go, but she graciously drove me from Riverside to Perris to board *el Corre Caminos* bus that would take me to Tijuana. Death and funerals in México wait for no one. Knowing quite well the Mexican custom of burying the bodies the next day after their death, I prayed with all my heart, "*Please, let me arrive on time to see her—I want to hold Mamá's warm hand; whisper my love and devotion. I want to bid her Adíos.*"

The pragmatic side of me prepared for Mamá's funeral. I packed a suitcase with mostly black, conservative clothes. Our family in México observes the ancient tradition of "vestir de luto", the wearing of black mourning clothes for a period of time in deference for the departed. On this urgent trip, I only planned to stay for my mother's impending funeral services—I was in no mood for visiting or sight-seeing. Therefore, I packed lightly, taking only the basic necessities (and cash to help with funeral expenses).

The flight to Obregón went smoothly and only took 90 minutes. Upon arrival, an ominous northerly wind chilled the February evening. Thankfully, my nephew Abraham met me at the airport and drove directly to the hospital. Looking out the car window, I recognized the familiar Sonoran desert landscapes. Meanwhile, my theme song played in my mind, "S*onora querida, tierra consentida.... Beloved Sonora, favored land....*"

At the Osorio Hospital, bed number 266, I encountered my Mamá intubated to life-support mechanisms. She looked pale and sickly— barely clinging to life. Mamá's infected, congested lungs were shored up by life-giving oxygen via a hospital ventilator. She was administered units of intravenous antibiotics and hydration.

Mamá was conscious and we made eye contact when I approached her bed. She managed a faint smile as I bent over the bed rail to kiss her forehead and embrace her with a loving *abrazo*. She couldn't speak because of the oxygen mouthpiece, but her eyes gleamed with *alegría* to see me. I exclaimed with delight. ¡"G*racias a Díos, Mamá*"*!*

Rosa Lidia was fortunate to have at least one loving daughter or son at her bedside at all times around the clock. My Sonoran half-siblings took turns holding vigil to care for our mother.

During this crucial sojourn I ate my meals and slept at my cousin Panchi's home on Calle Yaqui in Obregón. Every morning after breakfast, she drove me to the hospital. Fortunately, Mamá's vital signs began to stabilize and they removed the oxygen ventilator. One of her doctors suggested that we take a radio for her to listen to music —to help lift Mamá's spirits. It worked! So did our prayers for Divine intervention, including prayers to her favorite Saint, San Chárbel.

"*Qué gusto me dá que viniste, mijita*", Mamá whispered to me with a smile on her pale, still pretty face. In a soft voice, she expressed how happy she was that I came.

After 10 days of hospital confinement, Mamá began to ingest oral medications and small amounts of pureed food. Our parent/child roles reversed. As if she were an infant, we adult children fed Mamá spoonfuls of the sustenance needed to nourish her frail, sick body. Sipping through a straw, she drank water from a cup that we held for her.

My cousin Cristina was feeding Mamá breakfast when I arrived on the morning that she showed visible improvement. I noticed that color had returned to Mamá's cheeks and I told her, ¡*"Mamá, estás chapeada. Qué bueno"!* I recited the Rosary using beads I brought from home. It's made of Olivewood from the Holy land and contains a vial of blessed water from the Jordan River. Dora was so awed, that she rubbed the Rosary all over Mamá's body. Cristina lovingly gave me her own beautiful Rosewood Rosary that she carried. Later, when we were alone, Mamá shared with me that she had felt such excruciating pain the night before that she wanted to die. She begged God to take her. After praying to San Chárbel, she felt a hand press firmly on her forehead, and suddenly, the pain diminished, she said. "*Fué un milagro*", we concluded.

One day, Mamá told me that she had noticed that I wore a lot of black clothes. Amused, and with a straight face, I replied diplomatically, "*Si, Mamá... yes, I like to wear black. It's such a classic color that goes well with everything.*" I didn't want to reveal to her the truth, that I had brought mostly mourning clothes to wear at her intended Wake and funeral. It was then, that I knew that Mamá would recuperate—her keen observation skills returned intact.

Two weeks after Mamá's initial hospitalization, doctors declared that she was well enough to go home. The Hand of God prevailed through Divine intervention and prayers of the faithful. A skilled medical team, diligent family support, music, and Mamá's indomitable warrior spirit all contributed to Rosa Lidia's remarkable recovery from the brink of death.

La Fiesta

The 10-member *Mariachi Los Halcones* strolled into Mamá's humble home on Calle Cuauhtémoc performing her favorite happy tune, "*El Mariachi Loco*", the Crazy Mariachi. The Mariachi serenaded Rosa Lidia on the festive occasion of her recovery and homecoming. It was joyful! After a terrifying experience, my warrior mother returned to her family home. Mama sat stoically in a wheel chair listening to the Mariachi music and watching her family rejoice. Sentimentally, Mamá wiped tears of joy with the beige soft cashmere *rebozo* I brought her from Beijing a few years earlier. The lively music made her happy. Her spirits rejoiced to be home again, surrounded by adoring children and grandchildren. As my cousin Panchi likes to say, "*el pueblo Mexicano es muy pachangüero*"—the Mexican people like to party.

El Mariachi played Mamá's favorite tunes: "*Secreto de Amor*", "*La Negra*",

"*Caminos a Michoacán*". Dora requested "*Amor Eterno*", a ballad composed by Juan Gabriel for Rocío Dúrcal that lauds a mother's eternal love. I requested "*La Chancla*", a *Ranchera viejita* that was a favorite of my Nana Francisca. Rosa Lidia's kin were jubilant with gratitude.

Mamá evaded a close encounter with death. We thanked God for answering our prayers.

In the Judeo-Christian tradition, dancing is considered double-prayer. After having recited countless Rosaries, Novenas, and heartfelt *horaciones* for Mamá's healing, we jumped for joy—knowing our prayers were heard. We celebrated Rosa Lidia! Outside, on the hard-packed earthen patio, el *Mariachi* performed a medley of *Cumbias,* a fast-paced genre of Latino tropical dance music*:* "*La Loba*" y "*Las Hijas de Don Simon*" y más.

Rosa Lidia's devoted kin danced with relief to the spirited *Cumbia* rhythms. The dancing and singing helped us release the pent up stress, fear, and anxiety that had plagued us.

A spontaneous circle of dancing daughters formed during "*Juana la Cubana*". With appropriate abandon, we shook our full, womanly hips in the circular dance of joy. We shimmied our strong feminine shoulders to the rhythms. La Prenda, la Rosa, la Denise, la Fernanda, la Milagros, la Dora, la Elsa, la Chachita—we all danced with clapping hands and swaying hips. Flashing toothy smiles, we *cumbiaed* to the vibrant lyrics, "*Bailame suavesita, sabrocita, moviendo las caderas...*" With smooth hip gyrations and amplified shouts of glee, we paid tribute to nuestra Madre. We praised Mamá with dances and favorite songs.

With Mama's medical crisis behind us, and her full recovery on due-course, I made travel arrangements to return home, via Tijuana on Volaris Airlines. "*Gracias, Diosito Querido y Santa Maria, Madre de Dios. Sonora querida, tierra consentida...*". My now-lighter heart brimmed with gratitude—thankful for the fortitude and resources to traverse this difficult journey. Mamá was given a second chance at life. Providence offered us another opportunity to forgive perceptions of past offenses: *hija de la mala vida*. Old judgments and misunderstandings....

I felt gratitude for the reunions that emerged among our Sonoran family. My half-brother Saul had been estranged from Mamá for several years, even though he lived closeby in Providencia. The trauma of Mamá's near-death stirred him to visit her at the hospital to beg forgiveness (gracias a Díos). And, he joined us at Mamá's homecoming fiesta.

Graciously, my cousins Panchi and Lupe went to visit Mamá for the first time in several years. Amazingly, my 105-year old, beloved Tía Cúquita went into my mother's—her sister-in-law's—house for the first time in decades. We were overjoyed! Tía Cúquita and Rosa Lidia visited jovially, each of them in wheelchairs. Tía Cúquita made the trek to bid me farewell just an hour before I left Obregón for the airport.

During our visit, I taped an impromptu interview with Tía Cúquita as she spoke lucidly about her birthplace in Cananea in northeast Sonora where she was born in 1910. At the time, her father Ignacio Pablos worked in the copper mines near Cananea. Tía spoke about her family's return to Providencia, where my grandmother, mother, and uncle resided. Tía relayed how she met her future husband, José María Paredes Valenzuela—my Tío "Chémali"—at a dance in Providencia. Tío Chémali was my mother's older brother and only sibling.

Looking contented, Mamá quietly listened with interest to our conversation. She was happy to be surrounded by the people she loved—and who loved her back. "*Hasta luego, Mamá, no Adíos. Volveré a verte*", I declared as I left for the airport. *"I'm not going to say goodbye. I'll return soon,"* I promised my mother. The emergency sojourn to Obregón lasted only eight days, but obligations back home beckoned....

As destiny would have it, Saul died less than six months later following a brief illness in the same hospital where our mother had been interned. He is the third one of her adult children who has died. Otra vez, my Mamá's heart was crushed. In an attempt to console her, I opined that it was a Godsend that she and her son Saul had reunited before his untimely death. In retrospect, I'm glad for the opportunity to have seen Saul at least once more.

Diosito, about a year later, my beloved 106-year old Tía Cuquita fell and broke her hip. Sadly, she died from her injuries. I asked Mamá if they buried her in the historic cemetery in *Cocorít* where many of our family members are interred. She replied that Tía Cuquita's daughters buried her in a modern cemetery near Providencia. I lament that I'll never again see my beautiful Tía Cuquita—*la narradora del Valle del Yaqui*. She was a lucid, prolific storyteller. I feel blessed to have had her in my life. I appreciate all that she taught me throughout the years, since I was 9-10 years old. I am heartened to have a videotape of her vivid stories of her youth. As my esteemed Tía Virginia Vasquez would often say, "*God works wonders in mysterious ways.*"

Indeed, Rosa Lidia Valenzuela's motherland —*Sonora Querida*—is my second home. My sacred place evokes familial bliss—where I always return: "*Sonora querida, tierra consentida de dicha y placer...* ".

FIN

Note: My Mother, Rosa Lidia Valenzuela de Chan passed away peacefully on March 5, 2019—two years after this story played out in Ciudad Obregón, Sonora. I last spoke with Mamá by telephone the evening before on March 4th. I told her how much I loved her and asked her to hold on, as I was on my way to Sonora to see her. It was not to be. When Dora went the next morning to visit her at the hospital, Mamá died quietly. She is interred in a family crypt in Cocorít along with her cherished husband Federico Chan Ochoa and daughter Lorenza Chan Valenzuela. Nearby, her Mother Francisca Valenzuela Borboa, and son Saul Chan Valenzuela are buried—along with many other family relatives. Cocorít is a historic Pueblo Yaqui and one of México's *"Pueblos Mágicos"* because of the city's cultural, mystical, and historic fame.

DADDY .

by noelle marie falcis

what i remember : hemorrhage blurring fists to face .
my body ice ; my father's breaking . what i remember :
my voice a rasping screech , then silence silence silence
as i listen to his body splitting , fists to stomach , to neck,
to cheek , that cheek , i remember my mother kissing .
there were words , dirty words , angry blistering bawling
weeping hopeless deplorable words aimed like guns red
point needling at our chests . scream no my gut commands ;
nothing is what comes out . go to him my limbs implore;
but anchored are my feet on concrete . close my eyes ; no
don't close my eyes . witness . though i don't want to .

who it was : the blurring is white . it is multi limbed ,
and doesn't care that i am there . my father , his lips ,
curled to teeth , like rabid ~~fear~~ fury, fists balled, swinging
back, and losing . my father , he is trying . but the cold
hard logic enslaves his struggle . six fists are more than
two . three bodies are more than one . one manifestation
of brutal hate is larger than none . falling , his back bows .
his hands a helmet upon his head , cradling as they once did
me , shell to a gelatinous frame . his chest shudders like heartbeats
on his skin , the hands , they shake as those white men leave ,
the leaving as thunderous as when they came .

how it ends : the care . when i run to him , my seeing is

pushed away . then what i hear is un ending silence . i sit , hot asphalt warming thighs , and wait peer sweat glance and turn away . get up get up get up , i never say though i wish i did. when we leave for bahay , he drives two fists upon the wheel . we do not talk . i bite my lip ; whisper daddy and put one hand on cheek , that cheek , it will scar its breaking . his hand grasps mine , clamps on , clenches tight , pulls down , and our fingers entwine along the console . when silent steaming tears begin to fall , a fury ripens in my chest below the desert sun , no words come , but still :
my superman .

PAPAYA SOAP - IN FIVE PARTS

by noelle marie falcis

i :

in the tub , i sit upon its lip , uncomfortable and pouting . the steely enamel cold against skin , my skin , *dark* skin , forging bumps , rising like hills along my thighs . my palms are wrinkled wet , holding the soap bar aggressively in hand . the soap is a milk opalescence containing galaxies trapped in lye . it is bright orange like sun at its zenith . *likas* . it smells of disinfectant and processed papaya . it promises whiter skin – whiter, not lighter ; the marketing very specific . pale eggshell lines streak brush-strokes across skin , my skin , *dark* skin . bubbles frothing , bursting , disappearing . my fingers draw gardens along legs and my thoughts think zen : my finger the rake , the soap the sand , the skin the garden in need of rearrangement . of color , a more pure color . if my skin could be reshaped , redone , the imagining creating something better , more appropriate , much desired , then the soap , the papaya soap , is a cure .

ii :

there is mountain in my blood , the deep earth contained in arms and legs and skin inescapable . the farmer rebirthed across my many lives . this water reflects back a ruddy husk , like bark , too dark . it would not hurt so bad if inay did not look the way she did . if she was not as white as pearl , if she did not inherit chinese skin . if her skin , like natural skin , like islander skin , like our skin , darkened , this might not be a problem . but she is white . not light , but white , the better preference between the two . the white we so often wished we had . but what is left of my complexion shown through the water is tatay's skin : laborer's skin , somber , tough, too much spanish , too little chinese . that sad unfortunate skin . the skin that cannot escape itself . the kind that will never misremember because there are mirrors to remind you that fantasies are not real and your body and your skin will always remain : your body and your skin .

iii :

when i look at the water , there is a shift of chroma between calves and feet , the demarcation line of fantasy and reality . this garners disappointment so stark at the clashing of color . if a leg is dropped into water , it whitens and brightens . but when it is lifted , it is dark once more , white suds drifting then wafting to tub rim as if to solidify the erasure of possibility , all this white / right , you will never be or have . i drop my leg . lift it again . and what i have is always the same . light below ; dark aloft . why do i bother with any of this ? but theory and thought and intelligence and self esteem / love / worth is never enough . and so every night , here i am . scrub a dub a dub – how it haunts and grieves , a psalm of unmet hopes and dreams . i soap twice , thrice , hot water , scalding , may it burn all this dark , all this skin off of me . but when the mirrors unfog and i stand before myself. the skin . it is there . and still , it is the same .

iv :

on a hot spring day , i am determined . now is the moment when the cycle is to be destroyed . in bathroom , i rip doors open and slam cabinets shut . i seize packaging , slit plastic from product . *likas* in bulk is shoved in backpack and marched to desert where metal towers rise like rusted giants arching up to skies, landlines buzzing like buzzards in wait for prey . gripping soap bar after soap bar tightly in fist , i cock hands back and throw with vigor , violence , and velocity . the bars fly , ascending , and at the peaks of their arcs , the papaya galaxy and the crisp ultrablue of the afternoon sky is in perfect contrast , a millisecond of beauty . then the bars plummet to earth , disappearing into the terracotta desert . laying in solitude, somewhere , i don't care . i wonder if soap will dissolve , if , when it rains , the soap would disintegrate into runny white streams of balmy bubbles . if it would stain the earth white , if it would smell like disinfectant and processed papaya.

v :

here i make the tomb for islander marketing mirage gone bad to fade like dust in eternal barren wasteland . when the backpack is empty and all the bars gone , i am huffing and puffing and angry , sweat drizzling like juice , like life , like moist island lush against an infertile land . i fight an internal rage as my skin begins its own battle . i rip my shirt off and open hands to the air , to desert sky , my skin like offering , knowing the coloring will darken in a way that will take at least two winters to undo . the skin ignores this bit of practicality . i allow this act and i think it is grand , i think it holds meaning . i'm certain it is ceremony and i think i am free , but when it is all over and done and i am walking home empty handed , my shirt balled up in fist , alone in the desert , something breaks inside and then i am crying . i think this is loss . i think it is because i know i can't win . but also , i think that , perhaps , i can . and that , perhaps , in this one moment , i had .

A DAY IN THE PARK

by Rose Y. Monge

August 2017 Immigrant Story

It's June; the beginning of summer of 1956, and I'm eight years old. The family arrives in Fresno to pick figs at a new migrant camp. Our home this time is a long, narrow railroad boxcar moved from the railroad tracks and placed in front of commercial buildings near the downtown area. A high barbed-wire fence obstructs the view of the Holiday Inn. In the evening, I often hear the muted conversations and splashes of the swimmers. Loud, raucous, rock and roll music emanates from the pool area into the evening as the summer heat dissipates. How refreshing it would be to jump into the pool after a long day of picking figs!

On a Sunday and half-way through the picking season, Dad gathers us in the tiny quarters of the boxcar with an announcement. *Tengo una sorpresa, niños*, he tells us. *Vamos a tener un picnic como los gringos en el parque.* No sooner are the words are out of his mouth, all of us jump up and down with glee causing the boxcar to shake tumultuously. Ordinarily, our Sundays are spent sleeping-in, reading our DC comics or doing laundry. There are six other families in the camp and only one make-shift shower. Mom urges us to hurry and line-up before the hot water runs out.

I don't waste a second and grab my four-year old sister, Molly and dash for the shower. By 1 pm, all of us are spanking-clean and anxious for our adventure to begin. Elbows and legs bump noisily against each other as my four siblings and I scamper into Dad's teal and white Ford station wagon.

Ojos abiertos para una tienda, muchachos, Mom tells us. In short order, we locate a grocery store. Mom is pregnant so she asks my older sister, Trini and I to go inside with her while Dad tends to the other three children in the car. Our shopping list for our *gringo* picnic includes hot dogs, chicken, charcoal briquettes, Kool-Aid and ice.

As I walk in, I'm mesmerized. In addition to grocery staples, the store carries a wide array of toys, clothing, and toiletries. Shelves reach to the ceiling and overflowing bins with assorted knick-knacks placed haphazardly resemble an indoor maze. Mom cautions us not to touch or break anything as she goes to the market section. Trini quickly finds the lotions and perfumes leaving me all alone to explore. I'm fascinated by the blue, yellow, orange and red kites shaped like dragons reaching towards the ceiling. Suddenly, I catch a glimpse of the biggest doll that I've ever seen placed on the uppermost shelf. I strain my neck and stand on my tippy-toes to get a better view. Her hair is blonde, long and curly and she has enormous blue eyes that seem to follow me. She's wearing a blue and white gingham dress and carries a black, fluffy, puppy inside a small, white wicker basket. I don't know how I long I stand staring at her until Mom breaks my reverie.

Te gusta, verdad she asks. *Esta preciosa!*,

Si, mami. If I worked really, really hard this summer, could you buy it for me?

We'll see. We have to ask papi.

When, mami? When will you ask him? Can we ask him right now? I can go get him.

Well, if Yoli is getting a new doll, I want something too, my sister whines as she comes towards us. Dolls are for babies. I want some pink nail polish, red lipstick and some Evening of Paris perfume, she adds.

I didn't say Yoli was getting the doll, mom says firmly. *Vamonos*! I'm really tired and papi is waiting for us.

I follow her obediently, whimpering in silence trying to cover the emerging tears. Trini reaches out to hold my hand and as we exit, Mom notices my tears.

Don't cry, m'ijita. One day you are going to have a doll and Trini will get her Evening in Paris perfume. Now grab the bags and let's get this food to the car. The ice is starting to melt.

My tears subside as Dad drives to the park, but I still feel sorry for myself and angry at Trini for calling me a "baby." Dad parks the station wagon and finds a barbecue pit between two shady trees.

We scurry noisily out of the car and everybody has a job. I spread blankets on the grass for my one-year old brother, Ralphie and my sister, Celia who is two. They're in slumber-land in less than 10 minutes. As Mom heats the *ollas* of rice and frijoles prepared earlier in the boxcar on her trusty, propane Coleman stove, my brothers, Javier and Rodolfo observe Dad and soon take turns grilling the hot dogs and chicken. The tantalizing, savory aromas make my stomach growl. It's been hours since my *pan dulce*-my early morning breakfast.

After devouring our feast, we spend the rest of the afternoon exploring Roeding Park; walking near the lake and; and visiting the animals in the small zoo. Who knew there would be a carnival lighting up the evening skies? Dad treats us to the carousel rides and we end our day by splurging on Italian ice cream.

Overall, it is a grand Sunday being outdoors far away from the picking fields. While heading home, I can't forget that pretty doll. As I fall asleep, I'm still sad knowing I'll never have that doll. When we return to the store at the end of the picking season in August, she's gone. When Mom asks the owner about the doll, he tells her he has sold out. Of course, I'm dismayed but no longer shedding tears. I never ask my parents for a doll again and they never offer to buy one.

NOGALES IS NOT AGUA PRIETA

by Rose Y. Monge

August 2017 Immigrant Story

When are we going home? I don't like it here anymore, I complain to Mami.

I know, Yoli. Papi will bring us our *desayuno* soon, she says.

Well, I like it here, Trini chimes in. It's fun having picnics in the room. We never have picnics in Agua Prieta. You bratty kids are always whining, whining and whining, she adds.

Trini, please, Mami tells her quietly. Be kind to your brothers and sisters. Now, be a good girl and dress your baby brother. Ok, ok ok, she grouses. Mami is pregnant and is not her usual energetic self. Yoli, please look for my chanclas. I think they're under the bed, she adds. She rubs her tummy and asks me if I want a baby brother or a sister.

Do I want another brother or sister? Two brothers and a sister are plenty for me but I say nothing for I don't want to upset her. Trini, the oldest, thinks she knows it all and often bosses everyone around. Javier, being the oldest brother, wants to bully us as well and says everything we do is dumb and stupid. Rodolfo or Rodo is a sweet baby and too young to know what's going on. If I had to choose, I would like a baby sister who's just as happy as Rodo.

These last two days cramped into a tiny hotel in Nogales is not what I expect when Papi tells us that we're going for a train ride. Papi leaves early in the morning and I miss him. Mami tells us that he's completing paperwork for to us to go to California. I like Agua Prieta. Why do we have to leave?

It's the middle of summer and the room is chilly at night and too warm during the day. In Agua Prieta, I have the dogs, kittens, chickens and roosters to feed and chase around. And I like drawing, painting and learning new words at school. Sometimes, Papi takes us to the milpa. There's corn, tomatoes and peppers there and I can ride the burros. What can we do here? Nada, nada, nada. I want to go home.

Since Javier is still buried under the blankets, Mami gently jostles him awake. He grumbles, squinting his eyes as she hands him clean clothes. Rodo, notices that Javier is awake and gleefully leaps onto the bed. Giggling all awhile, he jumps up and down as Javier tries to swat him away. Giving both of them a stern look, mami says, please, m'hijos, I'm getting a headache. Rodo stops; sticks out his tongue at Javier before plopping head first onto the bed. I like Rodo. He's not grumpy like Javier.

By now, my stomach is growling. Pan dulce sure would taste good right now with some hot chocolate. We still have a jug of water but no food. While we wait for Papi, Trini and I straighten up the two beds. Mami folds clothes in the suitcase and then lays down. She tells me to keep an eye on Rodo. Javier and Trini join her on the largest bed to read their comic books. I try to keep Rodo busy and quiet. First, I read to him but he's too fidgety. Then, as I try to play jacks, he picks them up and throws them all over the place.

Seconds feel like minutes and minutes like hours waiting for Papi. Rodo is a handful and I'm at my wit's end when Papi comes through the door. We shriek in delight as he hugs us all in one big swoop. He has a bag full of bolillos, queso fresco, oranges and a bottle of milk. He checks on Mami as we greedily attack our breakfast.

Are we leaving soon, I ask Papi munching on my queso fresco.

Yes, m'hija, Your Tio Jose and Tia Louisa have signed all the papers to be our sponsors. We're going home tomorrow morning. And if everything goes as planned, we'll be in California by the end of the year. But today, we're going to celebrate. All right, m'hijos, what do you want to do?

Trini is the first to speak up. Let's go to a restaurant and have some enchiladas and churros with Coca Cola and then… No, no, no, Javier interrupts her. Restaurants are stupid. I want to go to the movies-maybe a cowboy movie. Can we do that, Papi, he asks. He doesn't answer but looks towards Mami who smiles and says we'll see. I don't know what I want but going outside to a park would be nice and having a cool, syrupy raspado sounds pretty tasty.

Hurry up and eat, m'hijos, papi tells us. Today we're going to get new passport photos. At last, we're doing something with Papi. And best of all, we'll be back in Agua Prieta tomorrow.

This is one of our passport photos taken in 1953. Javier, Trini and me (aka Yoli).

Mami is holding baby Rodolfo. She's pregnant with my sister Magdalena.

SAME BEAT

by Maria Mendez

How is it?
To roll in your bubbling blissful ignorance
Are you grateful?
For the womb that formed and warmed you
Can you endure it?
To know you've broken such a beautiful soul
Who are you?
To question a love, a life, a sanctuary
Betrayal
on your own
Bum, Bump
Bum, Bump
Do you hear that?
Bum Bump
It is the beat of my heart
The same as a black man
As well as one of a cruel tinted white man
Even the cream skinned grandmother down the street.

FATHERLAND

by Maria Mendez

Welcome
to the land of the judged
home of the scorned hearts
We accept everyone
Who is fair skinned
Who has emerald seeping from their fingers
Who's mother's hips cracked as they were
born in the so called "land of the free"
You are welcome
If you can pick a gender
If you love the opposite sex
If you let men do as they please
You want freedom?
You must fight.
Fight
With you mind not your knuckles
Fight
For those who can't
Fight
For those who have a voice
But are too afraid to speak
Fight
Against those who force your head down
Fight
Against those who shove silence down your throat

TOMB-SWEEPING DAY

by Emperatriz Ung

Daughter of Wong Sai Chuck;
resident of Riverside from about 1910-1916.†

清明节 upon us
Date of Death: —not specified
Returned to China: —unknown

who left Gom-Benn Village
it's all out of the database

we perform in your living room
fabricated dynasty long collapsed
those children escape you
the way you escaped Toisan

dialect lost, family name crumbled to
Anglophone sounds
brush strokes resist tradition

bloodlines weaken—
dilute responsibility

"12. Not all Chinese immigrants dying in Riverside were buried in the community. Chinese family associations, funeral organizations, and friends acting for relatives frequently shipped remains to China for interment. Some remains in Olivewood Cemetery were later disinterred and shipped back to China, according to cemetery records."‡

Harry W. Lawton, "The Pilgrims from Gom-Benn: Migratory Origins of Chinese Pioneers in the San Bernardino Valley," in *Chinese America: History and Perspectives*, (San Francisco: Chinese Historical Society of America, 1989), 69 †, 84‡.

AN INLAND EMPIRE BUILT ON ORANGES

by Emperatriz Ung

Inland Empire's
open hills, grooves
down the avenue

橙花 planted
at the heart
string transpacific lines
of fiction

who wouldn't want it
any other way when
the festival shuts down

city council cancels
no way to fill streets safely so
cut the violent street fairs
it all happens on humid nights

cool off under palms
leaves fan out to protect
color springs from cells
    browns the skin so
you don't want
    sun washed over you

scrub color off
under yellow light
believe—
    soap reverses
    pigmentation
forearm against forearm
shades change with seasons
where spring equinox melts
winter complexion
no umbrella no shade can shield you
from penetrating rays
embedded deep in DNA
color bursts into pulp

SCENT OF JASMINE

by Emperatriz Ung

茉莉花 knots in tangled soil
rough cement leave
behind sweet fragrance leaves
bitter tea

marchita todo lo que toca
Reminder that
Your lived experience is singular

feel sand stick to invisible film
you breathe—
in through all your senses

bamboo sea beckons
四川话 to ring from the terrace
and while they aren't 广东人
from your childhood
they love all the same

you are the 外国人
product made in America
shrouded in exoticism

gift for the ghost
白酒 warms lips
jolts the system

energy extends
below ground
combats impulses

MY IMMIGRATION EXPERIENCE

by Gudelia Vaden

My older brother, Pablo, told me that he and my father went to a field where he had planted some corn; the fields were called ejidos (communal lands) and he had another one where he planted beans, squash, tomatoes and peppers. As they dismounted from their horses, father walked ahead looking across the field and noticed the few greyish, green corns sprouting from the dry soil. He muttered a few words indicating that the rains had not come and there would be no corn crop. Father took a handful of the dry soil and threw it up in the air to see if it had any moisture. All dust blew up in the light wind. He muttered again as they walked back to the horses, and said, "vamos al Norte."

Pablo wasn't sure what he meant, but it was not good. It meant that we would be leaving our home in Calera for the United States. Mother had two little girls to worry about, but Father's worry was how to feed four kids and a wife.

We sold everything, including my dad's big sombrero. On the last day in Calera, Pablo had to get father out of the local cantina. He came down Cinco de Mayo Street, staggering with a pistol in his hand. We all climbed into an old, dusty black taxi and headed for Zacatecas to catch a train to Guadalajara and el Norte.

*

My immigrant experience began in 1946, when my family came to Riverside, California from Zacatecas, Mexico. I was in cultural shock, even at two years old. I missed feeding scraps to the chickens. I also missed my little straw chair that mom bought at the Mercado (market). This was one chair our burro had not gotten hold of. I kept the burro away by using whatever I could. But he was sneaky. Sometimes I wanted to shoot him, but he was needed for transportation and pulling the wagon. I also missed drinking the warm milk, just as it came fresh from the cow. All around me people were speaking a language I did not understand.

My parents, Vicente and Herlinda De Landa, and my three siblings and I came to live with my Uncle Reyes. He lived with his wife and numerous children in a two story white house on Sedgewick Avenue in Riverside. According to my mother, Uncle Reyes came to Riverside to escape being executed by the notorious bandit, Pancho Villa. The family lore goes that my very brave grandmother, Felicia, who was about four feet and a few inches tall, stood up to Pancho Villa, pleading for her son's life. They made an agreement, if she sent Uncle Reyes, who was 17 at the time, to the United States, his life would be spared. That is how Uncle Reyes came to the United States; before a blood-thirsty bandit could change his mind.

Riverside was a great place to be during that era; the air was clean and fragrant with the aroma of orange blossoms. The sky was blue all year round, except when the smudge pots' burning oil to keep the citrus trees warm, clouded the sky. There was also an abundance of oranges with orchards everywhere. My brother, Pablo, was nine years old. He would hop on his bike and bring sacks of oranges home. My oldest brother, Manuel, went to work on the railroad with my father. The work was excruciating and the hours were long.

After a year, my parents moved from Riverside to Planada, a small town in the San Joaquin Valley. My father obtained a higher paying job, as there was now a new addition to our family. Time moved quickly and it was time for all of us kids to go to school where we learned English. At home we spoke both English and Spanish, with the exception of mom, who only spoke Spanish.

My parents embraced the traditions they admired from the American culture while preserving much of our rich cultural heritage. We now celebrated Christmas and we no longer opened our gifts on the 6th of January, as we did in Mexico. Mom learned to prepare a Thanksgiving feast with homemade apple pie, while still keeping traditional foods such as enchiladas, tortillas and tamales. My parents still celebrated the Day of the Dead, but in a more subtle way; they prepared a small altar with pictures of the deceased and added favorite foods.

I finished high school and went to college. It was then I met my husband-to-be, Tom. We married in Merced and not too long after that moved back to Riverside, where Tom obtained a job with the Naval Weapons Center in Norco. To our delight we added a little girl and a boy to our family.

I am proud that my parents gave me a rich Mexican traditional heritage that promoted a bilingual, bicultural environment which has been of upmost importance in establishing my identity as a person. I hope to share my collection of family history with our children. This will also give them a sense of belonging, as it did me. It is my wish that all the cultures and languages come together to form a kaleidoscope of beautiful hues, colors, and song.

OLD IMMIGRANTS

by Hong-My Basrai

Mrs. Spring, their helper, came through my door with a cloth bundle, held hooked in her fingers through a tied loop. My ninety-year-old father shuffled in next, followed by my sister Anne, carrying his various suitcases, which she promptly deposited as I guided him toward the nearest seat. She promptly departed, leaving the two old refugees with me.

They had come straight from my sister's home, where my father lived after my mother passed away years ago. The arrangement had been perfect for both my father and Anne. He needed a family, and who else among his nine children, but Anne, would benefit most from his presence? He could help her with dropping and picking up little Pauline to and from school, and chauffeuring my niece to her extra-curricular activities when required. He could also manage Anne's dental office, doing payroll and keeping books—things he was good at in his pre-immigrant life. In fact, Anne needed my father as much as he needed her, and the timing of their co-existence couldn't have been better. His absolute confidence in her ability to balance her professional life with a young family boosted her courage to fight to have all, despite low morale periods when everything threatened to unravel. In his cheery presence, most impending disasters quickly dispelled.

He became Anne's right-hand man, and Mrs. Spring his right-hand woman, completing the household. Spring was her first name. Her last name was known only to my father who wrote her paychecks. She was their housekeeper and cook, there to round off the rough edges of their daily routines—keeping the house tidy, the three hot meals ready at specific times, an extra pair of eyes on Pauline, and reminding my father of his daily medication.

Erect of posture, with shining skin and jet-black hair thick in a chignon, she still retained some of her youthful look that, back in the former Saigon, had helped her snatch a husband as well as work here and there, now and then, enough to fill her children's stomachs and maintain a roof above their heads. After Vietnam was lost to the communists of the North, there were periods when she had feared they would all starve. While her husband traveled far and wide looking for employment—odd jobs or quick deals in the black markets—she had scraped together whatever meager possessions they owned toward a little operation producing steamed rice rolls for dawn's delivery to snack stands throughout the city. After a few hours' sleep, she would hop a bus to her next job at a government-owned co-op.

"At day's end," she recounted with a dry chuckle, speaking to me in Vietnamese, "Rice swept up from the floor was to feed five hungry mouths."

Her talent to transform virtually anything into nourishment might have been noticed, for the co-op made her their cook. "They pay little, but spoon licking I did, all day. I felt full just licking and sneaked home my share of food to keep the kids alive."

Decades later, the culinary skill that had saved her family brought her into my father's service.

She had come to the U.S. long after the first waves of Vietnamese *Boat People*, her story but another saga in the Vietnamese immigrants' record. It was for her the first breakthrough in a life of hardships and survivals. Her daughter, "the pretty one" had luckily met and married a Vietnamese American who had visited Vietnam for that specific purpose.

"She's done well," Mrs. Spring said another time, sitting up a little straighter with her nose pointing higher. "She was college educated. Sent us money."

Enticed by visions of easy wealth portrayed by her daughter, and the prospect of, one day, helping lift the rest of her children out of desperate poverty, she left her "mule-stubborn, dog-lazy" old husband for sunny California. For months she scoured Nguoi Viet, the Vietnamese-language newspaper, searching for ads placed by households all over Orange County seeking nannies, housekeepers, or nanny cum housekeeper cum cook; even for people like Mrs. Spring who couldn't drive, such jobs within the Little Saigon area were easily obtainable. Mrs. Spring had done brief stints in different homes, many of which were 3,000-plus-square-foot mansions in gated communities with hallways going different directions, marble floors that needed shining, dozens of sinks that needed scrubbing, and beds to be made with perfect hospital corners; not to mention grandmas who had to be pushed out into the sun and spoon-fed like children, with rich grandchildren too fast for Mrs. Spring to run after after their grandmas had dozed off, to keep them clean, well-fed, dandily dressed, to buckle into car seats several times during the day, and tuck into bed at night.

"Mercedes picked, then dropped me to my door every few weeks like a queen," she said, and in that rare intimate moment with her I detected a note of nostalgia for the good old, luxurious abundance befitting her imagination of how life should be in the United States. My tract home and dingy, dusty Honda Odyssey were quite a step down for her, but she endured. The reality was that, despite her working-buffalo constitution, only desperate households would hire a seventy-four-year old elderly woman to be in charge of their feeble, prone to falling grandmas, or run after precious little kids. She was hired temporally while people were waiting for a younger maid, only to let her go soon after. She sheepishly admitted, "Plus, I can't help my too-quick tongue. They half my age. Push me too hard, I fire back."

Many times, I had seen her snap at my niece. "Ask polite, I help."

She often corrected me in the kitchen. When I cooked Gujarati dishes, she held back criticism and stuck close to observe, clucking her tongue at the way I "kill green leaves," in her frank assessment.

Her fiery temper and strong personality—best qualities for survival in harder times—was not appreciated in the new land. People didn't want to deal with a sassy, troublesome household employee. Sharing a cultural background with her alone wasn't enough for people to disregard the fact that she was past her working age. What if she fell and injured herself in their house? Vietnamese Americans, even the ones who could afford to pay for legal hassles, had learned in time that their maids have rights and are not at their mercy. They did not want to deal with lawsuits.

It was Mrs. Spring's saving grace that she cooked the Northern Vietnamese dishes the way my father liked; and she cooked them well, giving the dishes of his childhood the same touch and flavor that reminded him of his mother's cooking, and home. Too often, his home of long ago was so vivid in my father's mind that, abandoning his meal half-way through it, he headed toward the door, if it would just open, if that pesky little Pauline would not sound her alarm. And Pauline's mother, that Anne. Was it her? In moments of lucidity my father used to talk out loud. *What a bossy daughter my wife had raised*! I understood his confusion: those same stern eyes, the same frowns and shrill voice that sent fear to his soul. *Or was Anne his wife? Hadn't she died? Why can't he go home?*

As my father's health drastically declined and dementia set in permanently, all three women became my father's guard. For Pauline, the roles had reversed. It was she who kept a close watch on her grandpa to sound the alarm each time he feverishly jingled the doorknob. After he had succeeded to wander into the streets several times, the logical plan was to move him and Mrs. Spring into my house, where I would provide additional supervision, until we could find a better long-termed solution.

My father was settled into one of the kids' bedrooms. Mrs. Spring set up her quarter in a corner of the family room. Her bundle of clothes that traveled with her from home to home as she switched jobs, neatly tied as if it was never opened, took no space, and except for the night when the sleeper sofa became her bed, the old woman, like her quiet, lumpy bundle, claimed no privacy and occupied no permanent space. She laughed at me when I opened the sofa bed for her to sleep in on her first night at my home.

"Please, Miss," she begged, looking at the queen bed with suspicion and embarrassment, "I only sleep on grounds." She proceeded to roll out the blanket that I had supplied her, plopped down like a buffalo with all her limbs tucked under her, shook out the piece of black cloth that, until then, was used to tie her belongings in, and shrouded thus in her own created darkness, said to me, "*G'night*, Miss. I up early for *yuh* father's breakfast."

Her love of cooking spilled into the love of grocery shopping. I would drive her to H-Mart and drop her there, as I drove my father to the nearest park for a walk. In the morning, she would do Tai Chi. When I asked her where she had learned the graceful movements, she proudly shared she used to demonstrate martial arts in front of a crowd. She showed me a picture of her younger self, in full martial garb, wielding a sword. She could also play ping pong with my once-champion husband.

Mrs. Spring's biggest worry was her U.S. Citizenship Test. When not cleaning or cooking, she would sit down with her Phillips DVD player, her N400 Test Questionnaire that included the 100 civic questions and 100 questions about the U.S. history, a white Olympus mini voice recorder, pen and pencil, and a notebook to learn her lessons.

I curiously looked in when she played her history lessons to see a map of the U.S., and a display of California's neighboring states, which reminded me of my children's third-grade social study. She pressed the voice recorder to her stone-deaf ear to listen to the questions, in original English as well as the Vietnamese translation, that she had paid a man with a fine northern accent and an acceptable English pronunciation to record at $50 a tape. She called him her teacher. Over and over that tape played American's basic knowledge and phrases.

How tall are you? I am five feet five.
What state has the most population? California has the most population.
What state is the largest state? Alaska is the largest state.

"Oi giao oi," she lamented in her thick Northern Vietnamese accent. "Nothing stays in this bull's head. I learn to answer one, another plain vanished. I stupid with English, Miss."

My family took turns quizzing her whenever we crossed paths. "How tall are you," we would ask, stressing *tall,* hinting. She would repeat our question one word at a time, searching her memory. After a while, she would say, dumbfounded, like a robot with missing chips, "W*ang piptee pao,*" causing the kids to bend over laughing.

Joining in their laughter, she admitted, triumphantly, "See, I hopeless," as if she had just scored a point over us, over our naivety, our ill-placed conviction on her ability to learn this torturous language. After having taught three kids to speak, my confidence suffered a hard blow.

She pronounced "states" as *schasche*. We tried correcting her, but we might as well have attempted teaching our dog to meow or contrived a leaky faucet to retain every drop of water. One day, exasperated, my Indian husband cried out in sing song English, "*Oye yay yay*, it's like me learning Vietnamese."

The insurmountable difficulty with the English language did not, however, deter the illiterate, old woman from devoting all her free time to the US citizenship questionnaire. "If I don't pass this year, I'll try again, until death takes me," she shared. Her fervor for learning was not due to patriotic feelings for the country that fed and housed her, and allowed her all available opportunities to progress economically and socially, nor was it due to any sense of self-worth, pride, or the love of learning. Her motivation was solely for one and only one thing: the monetary gain associated with that citizenship, that degree, that diploma—these terms were equivalent in her mind. At her age, she would be qualified for social security benefits if she could get naturalized. It would mean money for her grandchildren back home.

Alas, at the painful rate at which she was learning, her hard tongue chopping the soft vowels like an axe on wood blocks, she would never be "natural" at the art of becoming even a marginal part of the American citizenry. Short of a miracle, her thinking, language, habits, her tongue would always come in the way. She would never be assimilated.

"Study hard, alright?" I overheard her telling a grandson in Vietnam, a call she faithfully made weekly. "Chocolate, you like?" then, in a quivering voice before hanging up, "*bà* miss you," betraying a longing for her own flesh, the fruit of her womb's fruit; and home, the only home of all places on earth.

After these calls, she would return back to her lessons, and seeing me, let out a mile-long sigh. "Age money hard to earn."

Her stubbornness to pursue what she wanted reminded me of my father's own fights to conquer America. His last battle, right after his seventy-seventh birthday or so, was to renew his driver's license that DMV had revoked due to slow reflexes. He kept petitioning for one more driving test. Then, fed up when they refused to grant him yet another interview, he planned to change his name to Paul Smith. "Racists," he fumed. "Had I been a Smith they'd let me drive." That was the first and only time I had heard Dad complain of being discriminated against; my father had full faith in the justice and compassion of America. Thinking back, I asked myself, could it be, then, that Alzheimer's disease had loosened his tongue, freeing him to speak the dark corners of his mind, a decade before the first visible symptoms?

I had to let Mrs. Spring go a few months before my father's demise. By then, even her exquisite cooking could no longer help my father recall anything. He needed a man's strength to lift him in and out of his wheelchair and sleep near him at night, when he tossed and turned in Alzheimer's nightmares. She had come to pay her last respect, but we didn't get the chance to ask her about her citizenship test. A black Mercedes had whisked her off from the church, perhaps to the next place where she would deposit her humble bundle, and her valiant self, conquering the New World with her cooking, studying her test.

We wish her better luck next time.

WENT TO THE ARBORETUM TODAY

by Sheri Lindner

and marveled
at botany's lavish variety
azaleas and rhododendrons
at their full flowering
in shades of peach and raspberry
cherry and iced pink lemonade
and everywhere green
lime, forest, hunter, olive, emerald
I'd need a kind of Eskimo thesaurus
to find enough words
to describe the variety of hue
that finds home on the "green" palette
blanketing the earth
and pirouetting against the sky.
We wandered
the softened meandering paths
in awe of verdancy,
and sharing those paths
and sharing this reverence
were a man, his head swathed in a turban
like the white-starred petals
of the kousa dogwood,

a woman in a crimson sari
layered with the delicacy
of peonies,
a girl with cinnamon skin
taut and shimmering
as new birch bark,
another the color of rich spring loam
in which all this abundance
finds root
and we heard the cadences
of languages we did not know
and we understood all of it.

AUTHOR BIOGRAPHIES

Anthony Alas is a seven-times published author. His works have appeared in the *Pacific Review*, *In Parentheses*, *Scribble Lit*, and *Azahares Magazine*. After many years in New York City, Mr. Alas now calls California's Inland Empire home, again. He is currently pursuing a Master's degree in English literature, from CSU San Bernardino.

Angelica Maria Barraza teaches creative writing at Naropa University and is a counselor for a non-profit that supports homeless youth. Her writing has appeared in several publications, including *Bombay Gin*, *Cipactli*, *The Wall*, and *Helix*.

Hong-My Basrai is the author of *Behind the Red Curtain* (Los Nietos Press, 2020), a memoir about her seven years living inside fallen Saigon under communism. She was born in Saigon, Vietnam. At 22 years old Hong-My immigrated to Southern California. She speaks and writes Vietnamese, English, and French, and shares a home with her Indian husband who is fluent in Gujarati and two other Indian languages, besides English. Her three young adult children, when they are home, added to the cacophony. Hong-My is also a member of the Writer's Club of Whittier and PIVOT, The Progressive Vietnamese American Organization.

Raffi Boyadjian emigrated from Frankfurt, Germany as a young child. He lived in Los Angeles with one very thoughtful dog and another that was pure id; both greatly loved and greatly missed. He now (still) lives (in L.A.) with his wife and young daughter. He's a graphic designer by trade, a composer by heart, and a confounding writer. He was looking forward to getting a male dog to restore gender equanimity, but somehow ended up with an amazing female dog.

Minerva Canto is a journalist who writes short fiction and is working on a memoir-in-essays. "Dispatches: Tales of a Nomadic Journalist in Search of Home" relates her quest for home, identity and belonging amidst reporting throughout the United States and Mexico. She holds a B.A. in print journalism from USC and a MFA from University of Southern Maine's Stonecoast creative writing program. Born in Mexico City, she grew up in Santa Ana and lives in Corona.

Deenaz P. Coachbuilder, Ph. D. is a retired school principal, adjunct professor in special education and consulting speech pathologist. She is an artist, writer and environmental advocate. A Fulbright scholar, her poetry, essays and commentaries have been published regionally and internationally. Her two books of poetry, *Metal Horse And Shadows: A Soul's Journey* and *Imperfect Fragments* have been received with critical acclaim. Deenaz' paintings have been exhibited in diverse venues. She is the recipient of several awards, including President Obama's „Volunteer Service Award". She resides in Riverside, California, Seattle Washington, and Mumbai India.

Dr. Carlos E. Cortés is the Edward A. Dickson Emeritus Professor of History and currently co-director of the School of Medicine Health Equity, Social Justice, and Anti-Racism initiative at the University of California, Riverside. He has served as Scholar-in-Residence with Univision Communications and was the Creative/Cultural Advisor for Nickelodeon's "Dora the Explorer" and "Go, Diego, Go!"

Pati DeRobles is the 10th child in a family of 12, born in Mexico and raised in the U.S. She is a single mother of three biracial teenagers. Her oldest daughter just started Howard University, her son is a senior and her youngest daughter is a sophomore. Pati DeRobles has been in education for 23 years, and she has a doctorate in International and Multicultural Education.

Becca Spence Dobias grew up in rural Appalachia and felt her difference as an Appalachian acutely when she moved to Southern California. Her piece of fiction, an adaptation of a chapter of her novel, *On Home*, portrays a small piece of this experience and contrasts it with the experience of a first-generation Mexican immigrant. She is the mother of two young children.

Ellen Estilai, formerly executive director of the Riverside Arts Council and the Arts Council for San Bernardino County, has taught in universities in Iran and California. She has received two nominations for the Pushcart Prize, a nomination for the Orison Prize, and a notable essay mention in The Best American Essays 2011. Her work has appeared in *Alimentum*; *New California Writing 2011*; *Phantom Seed; Snapdragon; Ink & Letters; Heron Tree; (In)Visible Memoirs 2; HOME: Tall Grass Writers Guild Anthology*; *SHARK REEF*; *Riddled with Arrows*; and *Fiolet & Wing: An Anthology of Domestic Fabulist Poetry*, among others. Ellen is a founding board member and board member emerita of the Inlandia Institute.

Noelle Marie Falcis is a creative and an academic enamored by the intersection of narrative and performative praxis with cultural theory. Most interested in re-memory and re-imagination, she pursues storytelling through writing and movement. She uses these dual forms to understand the diasporic, post-colonized life, and how it affects her as a Filipina-American. Her fiction explores her heritage and the desert and city landscapes in which she grew up. Her work has been published in *Kartika Review*, *Hawaii Pacific Review*, *Riksha Literary Magazine*, and *VIDA: Women in Literary Arts*, amongst others. She is a VONA/Voices Fellow and Tinhouse Writer's Workshop alumna.

Natalie Hirt is a child of the Inland Empire, of Eastside and of Casa Blanca, of Riverside, California. She holds an MFA from UC Riverside. She has stories published and forthcoming in various journals including *The Wall, East Jasmine Review*, and *Sadie Girl Press.* She could forever live on a simple bean and cheese burrito, so long as it's homemade.

Judy Kohnen is from neither here, nor there. Raised in Canada, Iran, and France, she is a cross-cultural writer on themes of identity, loss and belonging. She escapes her suburban life by typing up stories…from her cemetery of unfinished manuscripts and poems, located in Claremont, California, under her bed. Her blog is www.judykohnen.wordpress.com. Judy is a member of the California Writers Club, Inland Empire Branch and also Chair & Community Liaison for local Refugee Resettlement Team #2.

Judy Kronenfeld is the author of four books and two chapbooks of poetry; her fifth full-length collection will be published by FutureCycle Press in February, 2022. She has also published short fiction, creative nonfiction, literary criticism and scholarly research (she won the UCR Distinguished Researcher Award, 1996-97, for *KING LEAR and the Naked Truth*, Duke University Press, 1998). Her poetry has appeared widely in magazines including *Cider Press Review, Cimarron Review, DMQ Review, New Ohio Review, One* (Jacar Press), *Rattle, Sequestrum*, and *Valparaiso Poetry Review*. She is Lecturer Emerita, Creative Writing, UC Riverside, and an Associate Editor of *Poemeleon.*

Sheri Lindner, Ph.D. is a clinical psychologist, poet, and essayist, whose works have appeared in many print and online journals. Her poem "Return" was awarded first place in the 2nd annual (2013) NCPLS poetry contest, and she has been nominated for a Pushcart prize. She is the author of *Opening Eden's Gate.* She and her husband do most of their living in Vermont.

Antonio Lopez holds a double B.A. in Global Cultural Studies and African-American studies from Duke University and is pursuing a Masters (poetry) at Rutgers. His honors include a John Lewis Fellowship, a Rudolph William Rosati Creative Writing Award, Lucille Clifton Memorial Scholarship to Squaw Valley, and nomination for the 2017 Nazim Hikmet Poetry Prize. He has attended numerous fine writers' conferences and his work has been widely published, including by *Pen/America, The American Journal of Poetry, Somos en Escrito, Hispanecdotes*—and more.

Jose Luis Lopez Jr. is a proud son of immigrants from Colima, Mexico. Jose is a proud father and dedicates his first-ever poem to his children, his nieces, and nephews. Never forget where you came from.

Juanita E. Mantz ("JEM") is a writer, performer, podcaster and USC Law educated lawyer and deputy public defender in Riverside. Her stories have been published in *The Acentos Review, Aljazeera, As/Us, The Dirty Spoon Radio Hour, Entropy, Inlandia* and *The James Franco Review,* amongst others. JEM is a Macondista and a VONA alum. She has a live video podcast based on her "Life of JEM" blog. JEM is finishing her memoir *Tales of an Inland Empire Girl* and is in the low residency MFA program at UNO. She serves on the board of the Inlandia Institute. Find her at juanitaemantz.com

Maria Mendez is an eighteen-year-old female in a Latin community. She has a voice and will use it.

Rose Y. Monge was born in Agua Prieta, Sonora, Mexico but has lived in the Riverside area since she was five. She is one of ten children-five of whom are educators. She earned a BA in French from UC Riverside and an MA in Education from Cal State San Bernardino. She retired after 41 years as an educator in the RUSD. She credits her parents for imparting the belief of the "American Dream" of unwavering faith and perseverance for success. Since retiring, she facilitates a memoir class at the Goeske Center and is a Board Member of the Museum of Riverside and the Settlement House.

Kimmery Moss was born and raised in Southern California. She was educated at the University of Southern California, graduating with a degree in Creative Writing and a minor in Political Science. She now enjoys living in the Inland Empire with her husband, two dogs, and four chickens.

Cindi Neisinger believes curiosity will lead you to your passions. She did not start off with the intention of writing. However, after many writing classes, throughout the Inland Empire, she was hooked. Currently, she is writing short stories and a screenplay. She also, serves on the Inlandia Institute Advisory Council.

Geeta Pattanaik was born in India, and has lived in Australia, Britain and the United States. Since childhood, she has loved to write poetry and paint. She works in oils and watercolors and was recently awarded Signature Membership of the National Watercolor Society. She was a finalist in the cover design competition of the *American Artist* magazine, and had work published in *Watercolor Magazine* in Summer 2012. She has had poems published in the U.S. and Britain and has published stories in Odiya, one of the languages of India.

Angelique Pivoine is an artist and illustrator living in Los Angeles. Her work explores American contemporary social and cultural issues through poetic lines and abstract figures of the faces, objects, and places she remembers—real, memorized, or imagined.

Linda Ravenswood (BFA, MA, PhD abd) is a Poet and Performance artist from Los Angeles. Committed to centering Women, POC, LGBTQ+, and traditionally under-represented artists and writers, Linda founded The Los Angeles Press (thelosangelespress.com) in 2018. She currently serves as editor in chief. Current projects include — *Qdias* — a mapping project for Asylum Arts (2020-2021); curating The GetLit Fellows chapbook project 2020-2021; Project 1521 (LACMA 2021); editing 8LA Poets (Hinchas Press, 2021); facilitating The Los Angeles Senior Writers Workshop; and producing a collection of poetry — *rock waves / sloe drags* for Eyewear London (2021).

Ivan Riascos is a visual artist who was raised in Central Florida and comes from a family of immigrants. His interest in photography and its role in history to create specific perspectives is the driving force in his artwork. He earned his BFA degree from The School of the Art Institute of Chicago, and his MFA degree from The University of Central Florida.

Emperatriz Ung is a Chinese-Colombian game designer, writer, & educator from the American Southwest. She works as a narrative designer for mobile games & is a 2020 Margins Fellow at the Asian American Writers' Workshop. She earned her MFA in game design from the NYU Game Center at the Tisch School of the Arts. She holds her BA in English from the University of New Mexico, and her MA in English Literature from Georgetown University. Find her on twitter at @mprtrzng.

Gudelia Vaden (Delia), a retired preschool teacher, has earned a BA degree in Liberal Studies with Bilingual-Bicultural Emphasis from CSU San Bernardino. Her immigration experience begins in the orange orchards of Riverside and continues in the fertile San Joaquin valley of Central California. Delia has returned to Riverside with her husband Tom where she has pursued her passion for Creative Writing. Delia has been published in the Inlandia Anthology since 2015.

Frances J. Vasquez is proudly bilingual and bicultural. Born in San Bernardino and raised in Highgrove, a citrus-growing enclave on the cusp between Riverside and San Bernardino counties, she is the eldest daughter of immigrant parents from México. Her mother is from Sonora and her late father emigrated as an infant from Michoacán during the Mexican Revolution. She attended local schools and attained BS and MBA degrees from the University of California, Riverside. An aficionada of arts and letters, she enjoys attending and organizing cultural events as is a Past President of the Inlandia Institute Board of Directors.

Leticia Velasquez is a substitute teacher, visual artist, and late blooming writer. She holds a BFA in photography from Parsons School of Design and a Masters in Philosophy from California State University Los Angeles. She lives and works in Los Angeles, California.

Anthony Victoria is a former reporter, who now serves as Director of Communications for CCAEJ. He's built a career on being the eye of the barrio. At a time when local news is underreported by major news media, as a journalist, Anthony helped shine a spotlight on Inland Empire policymakers and government agencies and their policy positions on immigration, homelessness, job-creation and public safety. He wrote about the growth of Latino-owned small businesses, the warehouse industrial complex, and the significance of community events like "Juneteenth" and the "March for Our Lives." His love and pride for the Inland Empire drives his advocacy and public service.

ABOUT INLANDIA INSTITUTE

Inlandia Institute is a regional literary non-profit and publishing house. We seek to bring focus to the richness of the literary enterprise that has existed in this region for ages. The mission of the Inlandia Institute is to recognize, support, and expand literary activity in all of its forms in Inland Southern California by publishing books and sponsoring programs that deepen people's awareness, understanding, and appreciation of this unique, complex and creatively vibrant region.

The Institute publishes books, presents free public literary and cultural programming, provides in-school and after school enrichment programs for children and youth, holds free creative writing workshops for teens and adults, and boot camp intensives. In addition, every two years, the Inlandia Institute appoints a distinguished jury panel from outside of the region to name an Inlandia Literary Laureate who serves as an ambassador for the Inlandia Institute, promoting literature, creative literacy, and community. Laureates to date include Susan Straight (2010-2012), Gayle Brandeis (2012-2014), Juan Delgado (2014-2016), Nikia Chaney (2016-2018), and Rachelle Cruz (2018-2020).

To learn more about the Inlandia Institute, please visit our website at www.InlandiaInstitute.org.

OTHER INLANDIA BOOKS

Güero-Güero: The White Mexican and Other Published and Unpublished Stories by Eliud Martínez

Care: Stories by Christopher Records

San Bernardino, Singing, by Nikia Chaney

Facing Fire: Art, Wildfire, and the End of Nature in the New West by Douglas McCulloh

Writing from Inlandia: Work from the Inlandia Creative Writing Workshops, an annual anthology

In the Sunshine of Neglect: Defining Photographs and Radical Experiments in Inland Southern California,1950 to the Present by Douglas McCulloh

Henry L. A. Jekel: Architect of Eastern Skyscrapers and the California Style by Dr. Vincent Moses and Catherine Whitmore

Orangelandia: The Literature of Inland Citrus by Gayle Brandeis

While We're Here We Should Sing by The Why Nots

Go to the Living by Micah Chatterton

No Easy Way: Integrating Riverside Schools - A Victory for Community by Arthur L. Littleworth

HILLARY GRAVENDYK PRIZE POETRY SERIES

The Silk the Moths Ignore by Bronwen Tate
Winner of the 2019 National Hillary Gravendyk Prize

Remyth: A Postmodernist Ritual by Adam Martinez
Winner of the 2019 Regional Hillary Gravendyk Prize

Former Possessions of the Spanish Empire by Michelle Peñaloza
Winner of the 2018 National Hillary Gravendyk Prize

All the Emergency-Type Structures by Elizabeth Cantwell
Winner of the 2018 Regional Hillary Gravendyk Prize

Our Bruises Kept Singing Purple by Malcolm Friend
Winner of the 2017 National Hillary Gravendyk Prize

Traces of a Fifth Column by Marco Maisto
Winner of the 2016 National Hillary Gravendyk Prize

God's Will for Monsters by Rachelle Cruz
Winner of the 2016 Regional Hillary Gravendyk Prize
Winner of the 2018 American Book Award

Map of an Onion by Kenji C. Liu
Winner of the 2015 National Hillary Gravendyk Prize

All Things Lose Thousands of Times by Angela Peñaredondo
Winner of the 2015 Regional Hillary Gravendyk Prize

www.ingramcontent.com/pod-product-compliance
Lightning Source LLC
LaVergne TN
LVHW052353100826
845147LV00013B/829

* 9 7 8 1 7 3 4 4 9 7 7 4 8 *